Mystic Tide

Angela Dorsey

Mystic Tide

Original title: Mystic Tide
Cover and inside ill: © 2007 Jennifer Bell
Cover layout: Stabenfeldt A/S

Typeset by Roberta L. Melzl
Editor: Bobbie Chase
Printed in Germany, 2007

ISBN: 1-933343-44-3
Stabenfeldt, Inc.
457 North Main Street
Danbury, CT 06811
www.pony.us

"Tallie, Tallie!" Erin called as she strode toward the fence. "Come here, Tallie!" The tall gelding shimmered orange-red in the sunlight as he raised his head on the far side of his large paddock. He started to amble toward her, his blaze bobbing up and down as he walked, then suddenly lifted his heels in a joyful kick and settled into a high, floating trot. Erin smiled as he pranced toward her. Talent always made her feel better, even when he wasn't trying. He was so beautiful, so full of life, so jubilant in his movement that when she watched him everything else seemed unimportant.

"There you are." Siobhan's irritated voice came from behind her, and a stiff mask automatically slipped over Erin's face. "What's taking you so long? We're all waiting."

Erin ground her teeth together. She'd never met anyone more obnoxious than her stepsister, Siobhan. How did her stepmom, Sylvie, who was such a nice person, ever have such an annoying daughter?

"So what are you doing anyway? Trying to make me late? Honestly, you're so passive-aggressive sometimes." Siobhan stopped beside Erin, her hands on her hips, and glared at her with narrowed blue eyes. "Well?"

"You must take after your father," said Erin sweetly and turned her gaze back to her magnificent chestnut horse.

"Why do you say that?" Siobhan's voice was suspicious.

"No reason." Erin ducked down to climb through the fence rails.

"No, I want to know why you said that!" For someone who wanted to be a calm, professional psychiatrist someday, Siobhan certainly spent a lot of her time angry.

"I'm sure with all your *knowledge*, you can figure it out," Erin challenged her stepsister. She ignored Siobhan's huff of indignation and greeted Talent with affectionate words. Unfortunately, she couldn't stop Siobhan's voice from invading her ears.

"You are so infuriating, Erin. I just don't know how to… you're such a…." Erin heard her stepsister's foot stamp the ground. "You're just completely impossible." Siobhan's voice broke off and Erin leaned her cheek against Talent's lowered head. The horse was her refuge, her escape, especially since Siobhan had come into her life. She glanced back. Siobhan was marching purposefully back to the house, probably planning to tell Sylvie all the horrible passive-aggressive things Erin was doing.

Erin had known the moment she saw her new "sister" that it would be difficult to actually *like* her. Siobhan was only a year older than she, but because of the massive amounts of makeup she wore and her sophisticated clothes, she looked a lot older. When Erin's dad and Siobhan's mom had married, six months before, it wasn't so bad because her stepsister was away at boarding school. Then Siobhan came home for the summer holidays.

Very quickly, relations went from bearable to terrible. Erin could've overlooked their different ideas about clothing and makeup. She could've dealt with Siobhan's snobbiness. Even Siobhan's desire to be a psychiatrist someday would've been okay, except for one small thing. She practiced analyzing everyone, all the time! She called Betsy, the lady who worked in the bakery, *narcissistic*, whatever that was; Sean, the local blacksmith, had *phobias*; the postman was *manic-depressive*, and on and on and on it went. It was slightly — though only slightly — amusing at first. Then Siobhan decided it was her duty to point out Erin's psychological disorders as well. She used passive-aggressive the most, but there were more. Erin's favorite was *raving lunatic,* something Siobhan had called her once when she'd been too angry to come up with one of her fancy labels.

She walked to the gate with Talent beside her, took his halter from its hook, and slipped it onto his head. "I want you to come inside while I'm gone, Tallie. I know you'd rather be out here, but I'd just feel better if you were safe in your stall." The gelding nickered and bumped her with his nose. "I know it's boring inside the stable. But…" She stopped. The feeling she'd had occasionally over the last few days was hard to describe. There was nothing wrong — other than Siobhan's presence that is — but lately, when she was outside with Talent, she got the creepiest feeling. It was almost as if someone was watching her. Someone with ill intentions.

Talent's shoes rang on the stone paved stable yard as Erin led him toward his stall. Even though she'd basically grown up in this stable, Erin still didn't take it for granted. She knew how lucky she was to have the beautiful, old building for Talent's stable. It was made of smoky gray Burren stone, the beautiful limestone found only in this area of County Clare, Ireland, and seemed almost alive with ancient grace and character. The ten stalls were roomy and well lit; the lofts were stuffed with sweet smelling hay. Erin even had her own "room" in the stall next to Talent's, with a cot, a tiny bookshelf, and a writing desk and chair. The barn cat, Cinders, slept on the little cot every afternoon and Erin kept all her favorite horse books on the bookshelf.

There was only one thing about the stable Erin would change if she could. She would add another horse or two or three. First of all, she'd buy Magic, the neighboring farmer's pony. Not to ride — she had Talent for that, and couldn't ask for a better companion — but to rescue. Magic had hurt his leg the year before and his owner had given the gray pony a year to recover in one of his pastures. However, Magic wasn't getting any better and Erin knew that his owner would be seeing that as well. Their neighbor was a nice man, but Erin knew he wasn't rich. Could he afford to keep Magic indefinitely? If not, what would happen to the sweet natured pony? Erin had approached her father, told him that with their family's riches, they could provide permanent homes for not just Magic, but for other horses who had fallen on unfortunate times. Her dad, however, was convinced it would be too much work for her and that her school grades would suffer. Both Sylvie and Siobhan had agreed with him, though in Erin's mind, Siobhan had no right to say anything.

She stopped at the door to the feed room. "Just a minute, Tallie. Let me get you a treat." The gelding snorted in response, his ears pricked toward the door handle. Erin laughed. Talent was still trying to figure out the door latch. She blocked his view with her body and opened the door — and froze.

There it was again: that horrible creepy feeling. The hairs on the back of her neck tingled as if someone was staring at the back of her head. The someone with ill intentions. She spun around.

Talent was looking across the stable yard too now. Her eyes followed his gaze to the loft above the stall on the end and, subconsciously, she moved closer to him. With his powerful shoulder against her side, she felt better. And the creepy feeling was fading now. What was wrong with her?

8

Why did she keep imagining these things? Maybe Siobhan was right. Maybe she was a raving lunatic.

"Mum, there she is. See? Fooling around with her horse when we should have left already." Siobhan's dark hair flipped around her head as she walked into the stable yard, Sylvie behind her. The smug expression on Siobhan's face made Erin feel instantly hot.

"Now Erin, you know we're in a hurry," Sylvie said gently. "If we don't leave soon, Siobhan will be late."

Erin turned away from the pair of them so they wouldn't see her sudden tears, and pretended to fiddle with Talent's halter. While Siobhan made her angry, Sylvie only made her feel sad. Not on purpose, Erin knew. Her stepmom only wanted her to be happy, and she was such a kind person that Erin couldn't help but love her completely. Sylvie couldn't help it if she made Erin miss her own mom, who'd died years ago. And that was another thing about Siobhan that bugged Erin. She didn't appreciate how nice her mom was. Her tears stopped as soon as her thoughts turned to her stepsister. Erin was glad. She much preferred being angry to being sad.

"I'm just putting Talent in his stall before we go. That's all. Siobhan's too sensitive."

Behind her, Sylvie sighed. "You know what, girls? One of these days, you two are going to realize you're not that different after all. Then who are you going to fight against?"

"No way! I'm not like *her*," sputtered Siobhan, sounding outraged.

"For once we agree," Erin snapped back.

Sylvie laughed. "And so it begins: the meeting of two minds. Now let's get Tallie into his stall. We have to get going."

So they were going somewhere. Good! Nicole was getting tired of the incessant watching. If the girl and her family were going to be gone for a few hours, she could have a nap. In fact, that would be a smart thing to do, Nicole decided. Especially since today, after an entire day around her stepsister, the girl might go to the abandoned cottage to recover her spirits — and then there'd be no rest for any of them for a while.

Nicole waited for the sound of their car to fade in the distance, then climbed down from the loft. She peered into the stall at the end of the row, but it was empty. Where had Robert gone? Surely, he wasn't bumbling about in the open somewhere. The family was rich, so they might have servants who would see him, and that would ruin everything.

The horse snorted, drawing her attention, and she noticed it seemed nervous. Could Robert be nearby? Slowly she moved toward its stall door. "You're an ugly beast," she said pleasantly to the creature. "I despise you, and all your stinky kind."

"Hey! Why are you mad at me?" asked Robert. He popped up like a bearded jack-in-the-box from the stall beside the horse.

"I wasn't talking about you," said Nicole. "Don't look so insulted. And what are you doing in there anyway?"

Robert disappeared. "Nothing."

She moved to the door of the stall to see the man sprawl back on the cot and pick up one of the girl's books. "Don't tell me you were in here reading," she said, aghast. "Even while the girl put her horse in its stall?"

"I was quiet." He flipped a page. "She didn't see me."

Nicole didn't know what to say. Was Robert really that stupid? Any one of the three, Erin, her stepmom, or stepsister, could have discovered him. And then all their surveillance and research and effort would be for nothing! Their entire plan would be useless.

Nicole spun away and stalked back toward the loft. It would do no good to yell at Robert, she knew. He would just say he was sorry a few thousand times and it wouldn't change a thing. And he was right — he didn't get caught. So she would do the smart thing and save her arguments for a time when she might actually make a difference.

But it was hard. So hard!

The day dragged on. Siobhan was acting in a play and, first of all, they dropped her off early so she could get ready with the rest of the cast. Erin, her dad, and Sylvie went to a coffee shop to wait for the production to begin.

Waiting in the coffee shop wasn't too bad. In fact, it was like the way things used to be, before Siobhan came back from school. Erin enjoyed hearing Sylvie and her dad talk, but didn't care about what they were discussing this time, so eventually her thoughts turned to Talent. She could hardly wait to get home and take him out for a ride. The day before had been rainy and cold and they'd stayed cooped up. It was just her luck that today was glorious — and it was being wasted on Siobhan's play.

Finally, they made their way to the theater, but arrived too early and had to sit for ages as the audience slowly trickled in. To pass the time, Erin daydreamed about the horse show being held in two weeks. She just *had* to do well. It was her first time competing in the more advanced Hunter classes and she knew Talent was certainly capable. The one she wasn't so sure about was herself, even though her riding instructor said she was ready. As long as she didn't embarrass herself, Erin knew she'd be happy. She didn't have to win or anything. However, in her imagination, she kept throwing Talent off his stride and making him knock down fences. Or worse, she'd fall off in front of everyone.

Just as she was thinking of ways to pay Siobhan back for wasting her precious time while she should be practicing the brush jump, the play began.

Erin expected it to be boring, even hoped it was in a way, but unfortunately, the play was funny. Siobhan was one of the main characters, and despite her best intentions, Erin was impressed with her stepsister's talent. On the stage, Siobhan wasn't snobby or irritating. She was hilarious, with a wicked sense of timing, and Erin found herself laughing despite her best intentions to remain disapproving and stone faced.

Too soon, however, the play was over, and then came the long wait for Siobhan to be ready to go home. They waited and waited and waited. Even Erin's dad became bored and stopped speaking for long stretches of time, and he was the second most talkative one in their family, after Siobhan. Most of the other actors and stage workers trickled out of the theater, and still no Siobhan. Just when Erin became convinced that her stepsister had snuck out in the middle of one of the larger groups, Siobhan came walking up the aisle toward them, her face alight with happiness.

"It's about time," mutter Erin. "Can we go now?"

But no one was listening to her. Her dad and Sylvie rushed forward to congratulate Siobhan, telling her what a star she was, and praising and fawning over her. Erin clenched her teeth. So what if her stepsister was a good actor? It didn't merit all this attention. A little voice in the back of her mind whispered that they would be just as happy for her at the horse show next weekend, but Erin shushed it before it became too loud.

Suddenly, Siobhan was in front of her. "So did you like the play, Erin?"

Erin shrugged. "It was okay," she said, reluctantly.

Siobhan smiled. "I knew you'd like it," she said in her smug voice.

"Yeah, all that waiting was pretty good. It was the part in the middle that was boring, when all those losers were running around on the stage," said Erin.

Immediately, she wished she could take back her words. She hadn't meant to sound so cruel. Horrified, she saw tears spring into Siobhan's eyes. But why did her stepsister have to take everything so seriously? Why couldn't she see that Erin was just upset because she had to wait so long?

"Erin, I can't believe you just said that. What's wrong with you?" said her father from behind her, displeasure thick in his voice. "Siobhan was wonderful, and I know you enjoyed the play."

"That's... that's okay," stuttered Siobhan. "I'm sorry you had to wait. I tried to hurry. Really."

Erin felt even worse. Now her stepsister was apologizing to her! *But she's an actor, and she's just acting now,* Erin decided firmly. *She really doesn't feel hurt. She wants me to feel bad, that's all.*

"Let's go, everyone," said Sylvie, tenderly. She put her arm around her daughter. "You were so good, honey. And we're *all* so proud of you."

"We certainly are," added Erin's dad. Stiffly, he turned to walk after his wife and stepdaughter, leaving Erin to follow alone.

"Whoa, Tallie." Erin reined the chestnut gelding to a halt. The abandoned cottage stood before them, the gray stone walls strong and indestructible, with gaps where the windows and door had been. Her father had long ago forbidden her to come here, not because it was dangerous, but because it was private property and he didn't want her to trespass. However, the fact that the place was deserted was part of the reason Erin liked it and she came often, especially lately. She could be alone here. The owners lived in Dublin and hadn't been back to visit for at least a year.

She drew in a deep, trembling breath. Finally, she could cry if she wanted. No one would see her tears here. This place was worlds away from the suspense of the silent drive home, away from the disapproving, unhappy look on her father's face. The expression on Sylvie's face had been kinder, more compassionate, but that had been even harder to bear. And Siobhan, well, Erin hadn't wanted to even look at her. Everything was her fault.

She turned in the saddle. Beyond the stone fence that circled the cottage, past the single tree that stood to one side of the ungated opening, the naturally formed pavements of the Burren stretched away into the distance. The stones shone like huge glossy bricks edged in green. It was a perfect day, warm and still under the late afternoon sun. Too bad Siobhan had ruined it for her. Erin ran her fingers through her short, reddish brown hair, sighed, and dismounted.

The gelding nickered, and nuzzled her sympathetically. Immediately, Erin felt her eyes sting with tears. Talent was the most understanding horse in the world. She swallowed noisily and reached up to straighten his forelock. "Today I made a mistake and now everyone's mad at me, Tallie," she whispered. "I don't know how to make it right with Dad and Sylvie."

Talent moved to rest his head on Erin's shoulder. His dark eyes stared into hers, and in their depths she could see her own tear streaked face. She dashed the droplets away, and when more ran down her cheeks she moved to Talent's side to wipe her face on his silky neck. "I know it's mean to say this, Tallie, but I just wish Siobhan would go back to her stupid boarding school. I like it when it's just me and Dad and Mum." She shook her head. "I mean, Sylvie."

A preoccupied look crept over Erin's face as she unclipped one end of Talent's looped reins and turned to sit against the stone cottage wall. Was that part of the reason Siobhan was nasty to her so often? Because Erin was taking a share of her mom's attention? And was that why the mean words had sprung from her own mouth — because she was mad at the way Sylvie and her dad were flattering Siobhan? Were she and Siobhan *competing* for their parent's affection? But that was something little kids did. Erin scowled. What a stupid idea.

Birds were singing like mad from the branches of the ancient tree, and the sun felt comforting on her skin. The refreshing breeze smelled of wildflowers. She closed her eyes and tipped her head back so the sun was glowing full on her face. There was a slight tug on the reins and she heard Talent take a bite of grass, then chew rhythmically, serenely. She sighed again. It felt so good to be away from the confusion that was home these days.

After a few minutes, she opened her eyes to watch the red gelding. Talent's ears swiveled toward her, but he didn't stop grazing. Erin sighed contentedly. At least, when she was with Talent, everything was all right. She was sure that without him to listen to her and carry her away from her problems, she'd have gone crazy by now — and then, of course, Siobhan would label her insane.

Or maybe the technical term is nuts, or batty, or bonkers, thought Erin and kicked some stones lying in front of her. One of them went spinning toward Talent and the horse raised his head and snorted.

"I'm so sorry, Tallie," said Erin, leaping to her feet. Now Siobhan was making her be cruel to her horse! "Come on, let's get out on the green road. I have to feel some wind on my face."

She clipped the rein to his bit again, then gently pulled down to loop the leather over his head — but Talent kept his head high. In fact, he wasn't even looking at her. Instead, his attention was directed behind her.

"What is it, boy?" asked Erin, turning back to look at the abandoned cottage. "What do you see?" Nothing was there. She looked back at the horse. He was still staring at the stone corner of the cottage. Was someone behind the old building?

Talent snorted, and his hoof struck the ground. Once. Twice. Then he pinned his ears and pranced sideways, his head even higher. Fear spiked Erin's heart and she froze. Were the cottage's owners back? Were they wandering about their property, making sure everything was okay? What if they told her dad?

But surely, even strangers wouldn't make Talent act so nervous.

"Oh, no," Erin whispered. There was only one thing Talent had ever been afraid of. The neighbor's bull. He must be loose!

She reached for the stirrup. "Hold still, Tallie," she begged, breathless with alarm. "We have to go! Now!" Talent caught the panic in her voice and danced away, almost jerking the rein from her hand.

Erin took a deep calming breath. She would get nowhere with the sensitive horse if she kept acting like a terrified fool. "I'm sorry, Tallie," she crooned, holding the rein with a firm grip and forcing the tremor from her voice. "Just be calm. Everything is okay. Now let's just go for that ride, okay?" With her hand out, she approached her horse, first stroking his nose, then his neck. She was just about to put her foot in the stirrup when Talent snorted loudly and leapt away again.

"Tallie?" And that was all Erin had time to say before she was seized from behind. One arm wrapped around her arms and midsection, immobilizing her, and a strong hand clamped over her mouth, stopping her from crying out. Then she was dragged backward, kicking and squirming, into the abandoned cottage.

"Stay here," Nicole said to Robert. "Keep her out of sight, and I'll take care of the horse." She grabbed the cloth bag of grain she'd prepared and hurried after the animal. It was already on the other side of the old stone fence, circling the tumbledown structures with an animated stride, its reins flapping around its front legs. Why did she always get the tough jobs? If Robert could be trusted to do something right, he would be doing this right now.

"Relax," Nicole muttered to herself. She had to calm down or the horse wouldn't let her near it. "Tallie, Tallie," she called out in the singsong voice she'd heard the girl use when calling her horse in from the pasture. The call worked. The red horse stopped and looked back curiously, then gave a thunderous snort that rang across the Burren hillside.

"Tallie, Tallie," Nicole called again, shaking the cloth bag of grain. The morsels rattled dryly in the sack, and the horse pricked up its ears. "You're a big scary one, aren't you?" Nicole said in a sweet voice and climbed over the stone wall. Closer, closer she walked. The horse took a nervous step back, and Nicole stopped. Waited. She had to be patient, wait for it to settle down. Catching the horse was essential to their plan.

"What's taking so long?" Robert called from the cottage doorway.

21

Nicole turned to see him watching her, the girl firmly in his grip. Was he an idiot, yelling like that? Didn't he see the horse was already nervous without him bellowing irrelevant questions at her? She made a sudden chopping motion with her hand — shut up! — and adjusted her expression before turning back to the animal.

"Come here, you ugly beast," she murmured pleasantly. "Just let me catch you for a minute. Then you can run to safety and abandon your owner."

Honestly, she'd never understood why some people liked horses so much. They were big and smelly and dangerous. They'd kick you or bite you or run away with you every chance they got. Worst of all, though, they had no loyalty whatsoever. She'd take a dog over a horse any day.

"Now, now, Tallie," she said, her voice smooth and sugary as can be. "That's a rotten fellow. Just let me pin this to your saddle pad thing and put your reins over your neck, and you can be on your cowardly way."

Through a fog of fear, Erin watched the wild haired woman edge closer and closer to Talent. What did these people want with her and her horse? What were they going to do to them? What if they hurt Talent?

In desperation, she tried wiggling out of her captor's grasp. Talent wasn't caught yet. If she could just warn him…

"Just hold still now," said the man pinning her. His voice was deep, slow, and relaxed, as if he was spending a day at the beach instead of restraining someone against their will. "Nothing bad's going to happen if you do what we say."

Erin rolled her eyes up, straining to see her captor, but all she could see was the bottom of a dark bushy beard. She turned her attention back to Talent and the woman. She was at the gelding's side now. As Erin watched, she stroked his neck and then grabbed the reins.

It still isn't too late for Talent to pull away, Erin realized. *I have to do something. Now!* She lifted her leg and brought her foot down hard. Her riding boot heel made contact.

"Ow! That hurts!" The man sounded like she'd hurt his feelings more than his foot.

Erin slammed down her foot again, but the man simply held her harder against his chest, turning her head to the side so she couldn't see her beloved horse anymore. Tears of fear and frustration sprung from Erin's eyes. She was so helpless.

So vulnerable. And she could no longer see what the woman was doing with Talent!

"Sorry. I don't want to hurt you. I just need you to hold still, that's all." A pause. "Will you hold still?"

Erin tried to nod her head, and he must have felt her attempt to move. His hand loosened, allowing her to straighten her head. And she could see the woman, striding toward the cottage. But no Talent.

"I can let you go if you promise not to run."

This time Erin could nod, and the man slowly released his grip. He pointed toward the back wall. "Go back there."

"But my horse," Erin managed to choke out.

"Don't worry. He's on his way back to your house."

Erin sagged to the ground in relief. Talent was safe.

The shaggy haired woman stepped inside the building, pushed her long bangs from her face and stared at Erin as if she were a mere curiosity. "She giving you any trouble?" she asked the man.

"Just crying, that's all," the man responded. "You know how I hate that. It always makes me feel mean."

"You'd better let me go," Erin blurted to the woman. "My dad will call the police as soon as Tallie gets home without me."

The woman looked at her with indifferent eyes. "He won't be calling anyone." She went to a backpack leaning against an inside wall, took out a baseball cap and threw it on the ground in front of Erin. "Put this on."

"No."

"What did you say?"

Erin stuck her chin out. "I don't want to put it on. And you have no right to keep me here. You'd better let me go." If only her voice wasn't trembling, making it obvious that she was afraid.

24

"You're not going anywhere, *and* you're wearing the hat." The woman advanced as she spoke. "We can do this one of two ways. Easy or hard. It's up to you. But either way, you'll be wearing the hat when we leave this cottage."

"Please. Put on the hat," the man begged.

It was more the man's unexpected kindness than the woman's threats that made Erin reach out and take the hat in her hands.

A condescending smile touched the woman's face. "Bright girl."

Erin slid the hat onto her head. It was too big and flopped low on her brow. She peered at her captors from beneath the brim. "What are you going to do with me?" she asked, trying to sound braver than she felt.

"Use you, darling," the woman said, and a touch of a foreign accent crept into her tone. "You're going to make us rich. Now just sit back and rest while you can. We'll be leaving soon."

Talent. Stop! It is I, Angelica!

Thank you, my friend, for calling me to help you. Now please, try to be calm. You must tell me what has happened. You must tell me why you were galloping across such rough terrain, panic stricken and alone.

Strangers have taken your girl from you? One of them approached you and you let her, because you thought she might allow you back to your girl. But instead, she merely pinned an object to your saddle pad? Hold still, my dear. Let me look.

Oh my! It is a ransom note. The strangers who stole your girl will not return her until they have been given a great sum of money!

Come Talent, let me climb onto your back. We will hurry to your home at a safe speed, for your girl's parents must receive this note. Then, when they have been alerted, we will return and see what we can do to help her.

The woman peered out the door. "It's almost sunset. All the hikers will be setting up camp for the night now. We can go."

The man merely grunted. He was reading a book from Erin's stall bookcase — one of her favorites, Erin noticed with dismay — and was leaning against the wall, completely engrossed in the story.

Seconds passed in silence.

"Come on. It's time to go."

"I'm almost done." The man flipped a page.

"You know we decided to leave just before sunset," The woman spoke slowly and clearly as if she was trying to explain something to a young child. "That way we can get the farthest before night falls, and the chances of someone seeing us are the lowest."

"I just need ten more minutes."

"No! We go now."

The man seemed unfazed by her orders. "Ten minutes."

The woman stood silhouetted against the doorway of the abandoned cottage with her fists clenched, her anger barely under control. Abruptly, she leapt to the man's side, snatched up Erin's book, and flung it against the back wall of the cottage.

"Hey, Nicole, what'd you do that for?" the man asked. He raised his bulk to a standing position.

With a cry of frustration, the woman grabbed his arm

and jerked him out of the cottage. They stopped just outside the door. "You idiot! Remember what we discussed?" The woman's whisper carried on the still air. "About not saying our names in front of her? So *think* before you blurt things out."

"Sorry," the man mumbled. "I forgot. It won't happen again. Sorry."

"It better not. And we're leaving. Now!"

"Okay. Sorry."

Erin kept her eyes down as the two adults re-entered the cottage. She didn't want them to think she'd been listening, but she remembered the name the man had said, and the woman's — Nicole's — reprimand only highlighted how important it was that she keep her eyes and ears open.

"Get up," Nicole said, and Erin reluctantly climbed to her feet. "We're leaving."

"Where are we going?" asked Erin, as the man walked past her and picked up the book. He dusted it off and shoved it into his backpack.

"I'll lead the way," Nicole said to the man, ignoring Erin's question. "And you," she said, turning back to the girl. "Follow me. If we meet anyone, you don't say anything. Not a word. You understand?"

Erin nodded stiffly.

"And don't look so scared," Nicole added. "If you do what we say, and if your family pays the ransom, you'll be home by tomorrow night."

Erin nodded again, and with her head down, meekly followed Nicole from the cottage.

However, once she was outside, an almost overwhelming desire to run coursed through her body. The Burren stretched away, lonely and sparse in every direction. If she could just run fast enough… somehow dodge their grasping hands… if

Talent was still around somewhere and she had time to climb into the saddle… She searched the expanse but didn't see him.

Then she heard the man's step behind her. She swallowed nervously. He was much stronger and faster than she was, and an escape attempt now would surely end in failure. She would be much smarter to wait for a less risky opportunity to get away.

And if she found no safe way to escape, she would be wise to do exactly what Nicole and the man told her to do. No matter that it hurt her pride. No matter that her dad had to pay lots of money. Getting home safe was the most important thing.

Ah, this is your house, Talent. Good. Stop and I will slide from your back. Now go to the front entrance and call them.

There he goes. He gallops toward the house at full speed and slides to a stop at the massive door. Then he calls, loud and long. His cry is filled with the pain of his loss. It sears my soul. What distress! What fear for his girl!

And the door opens. A girl emerges, a sister? She must be. However, she seems afraid of Talent, stepping back as he approaches her. Now a man comes out of the house. There, he has the note, and is reading it. He is running back inside!

Now that they know, Talent and I can pursue our undertaking. He trots toward his stable, out of sight around the corner of the house. I will meet him there.

At first they hiked straight away from the cottage, across the wild Burren. Erin had to concentrate on where she was stepping. The pavements looked smooth from a distance, but in reality they were rough and pitted. The grykes, fissures in the limestone that sometimes stretched for hundreds of feet, became both deeper and wider as they walked, and she could hear water running through the narrow crevices. She licked her lips. She was getting thirsty. Should she ask her kidnappers for water?

A stone shifted underfoot and Erin lurched forward. She hit the rocky ground with a gasp. "Ow, ow, ow," she whispered, and pushed herself into a sitting position. Beads of blood were forming on her palms.

"Get up," Nicole nudged her with the toe of her hiking boot.

"Let me see," the man said, and bent over Erin. Erin held out her trembling hands, palms up. After a quick look, he shrugged off his backpack and took out a compact first aid kit. He opened a sealed packet and took out a moist towelette. "Here," he said, handing it to Erin. "You can wash it with this."

Erin dabbed at the dirt in the scrapes until they were relatively clean.

"Throw it under here," commanded Nicole, and Erin looked up to see she'd turned over a stone. She tossed the cloth beneath it and the woman neatly flipped the rock back over it. "Now let's get moving."

"Can I have a drink of water first?" asked Erin, taking her courage in hand.

The man passed his canteen to Erin, and she drank deeply. She was so thirsty. When she was done, she handed the canteen back. "Thanks," she whispered.

"No problem," the man said, pleasantly. He took a swig from the canteen as well.

As they started walking again, Erin looked forlornly about. The sun was on the horizon now. Surely her family had found the note on Talent's saddle pad and were on their way to rescue her. But then, how would they track her across this stony ground? How would they even know where to start looking? She wasn't allowed to go to the abandoned cottage, so they wouldn't think of starting there. And according to Nicole, the note said not to contact the police, so they wouldn't have any help.

The only one who knew where she'd been kidnapped was Talent. Maybe, once it got dark, he would come to rescue her. He was a smart horse, and Erin was certain he knew she was in trouble. He'd want to help her. In her mind's eye, Erin imagined slipping away from the kidnappers under the cover of night, hurrying across the Burren, and seeing Talent loom up before her. She would climb onto his powerful back, and away they would race, leaving Nicole and her partner far behind.

"Finally," Nicole said, jerking Erin's attention back to reality. She stepped out on the "green road," one of the ancient grassy roads that wove through the Burren. "Now we can really make good time."

Erin too, breathed a sigh of relief. The green roads were much easier to walk than the rocky Burren pavements. But there was another, even better thing about the green roads — they were traveled by hikers. There was a chance they'd come across someone who could help her.

And in case they did, she should be prepared.

As if she'd read Erin's mind, Nicole turned to her. "If we meet anyone, don't say a word. I don't want to use this, but I will if I have to!" She patted her right jacket pocket, revealing a bulge. A gun? It had to be. Nicole was armed!

With a sinking feeling Erin realized it would be too dangerous to call out for help. She had to let any passing hikers know she was being kidnapped without her kidnappers knowing what she was doing. It would be hard to do, but somehow she had to wordlessly tell them to not try to save her right then. Instead, they'd have to pretend they didn't know what was happening, and once Erin and the kidnappers passed by, use their cell phone — if they had one — to call the police. But how was she to communicate so much without saying a single word? Or without the kidnappers understanding what she was doing?

And there was another problem. The sun was setting. A pink glow spread across the gray stone all around them, and the tiny alpine plants that flourished in every crevice were alight with the sun's last rays. If they were going to meet anyone, it had to be soon.

As if on cue, she heard distant voices. Instantly, Nicole spun around to face her. Erin stopped short, and the woman leaned close to her ear. "Say nothing," she hissed. "You understand? Nothing. Or else you'll be sorry, and so will they."

"Don't worry. She won't say anything," the man said, in his deep, slow voice. "Will you?" he asked Erin.

Erin didn't know what to say. Of course she would, if she thought it would help her escape.

"Quiet now," Nicole whispered, and turned around. "They're coming."

33

Talent, this must be the place they stole her from you. Fright hangs in the air like a fog in this place.

We must not linger. I will track her into this rock wilderness, following her life force even though I find it difficult to open myself to her fear.

Come, let us hurry!

Beyond Nicole, Erin could see two people hiking toward them along the green road: an older man and woman. As they drew nearer, she could tell that the couple must either be locals or travelers staying overnight in the area. They didn't have any camping gear with them, only daypacks. Binoculars hung around each of their necks. Instead of looking at Erin and her kidnappers as they approached, the couple seemed captivated by the beautiful rocky vistas stretched beneath the sunset.

"Hello," said Nicole, politely, when they two groups came together.

"Good evening," said the woman walking in front, then her gaze swept back to the scenery. Erin slowed and tried to speak through her eyes as the stranger strode past, but the woman didn't even look at her.

Then the male hiker was passing Nicole. He nodded to her… and his eyes slid on toward Erin… This was her chance!

"Great evening, isn't it?" The voice boomed behind Erin.

The older man's gaze skipped past Erin and he smiled at her kidnapper. "It surely is," he replied. "A grand evening to be sure." And then he too was past and striding onward.

Erin's body shook with her desire to run after the hikers, to scream and beg for their help. She had to try — she couldn't bear just walking on, calmly and casually, as if nothing was wrong!

She took one step, then the thought of Nicole's gun made her hesitate. As if he knew what she'd been about to do, the man's two large hands came down, one on each of her shoulders. "Don't even think about it," he said, his voice strident in the stillness.

"Is everything okay?" A distant voice.

"Just fine," Nicole yelled to the hikers. "Our little sister's tired, that's all. But don't worry. We're almost back to our camp."

Erin realized that the hikers had stopped. The male kidnapper's voice must have alerted them. She longed to scream to them, "Help me!" But she didn't dare, and then it was too late. They were already turning around. They were already striding away.

"Sit down on this rock," the man said, and this time his voice was much quieter. Erin sat, clasped her shaking hands together, and blinked back sudden tears. She'd come so close to being rescued, or at least discovered. She stared longingly after the retreating couple. Maybe, just maybe, the hikers *hadn't* believed everything was fine. Maybe they were just acting nonchalant as they hiked away, thinking they'd phone for help as soon as they were out of sight. But even as the notion crossed her mind, she knew it was hopeless. Unless the hikers were as good at acting as Siobhan, there was no chance. They probably believed she was out hiking with her big brother and sister, and was tired — just as Nicole said.

There was a long silence as the kidnappers waited for the couple to hike farther away. Erin wished she could just sink down into the rock and disappear. Somehow the man had sensed she was about to run, despite Nicole's gun. Now what would they do to her? Would they punish her?

"Couldn't you have said it a bit quieter," Nicole spat out.

The elderly couple must be out of earshot now. "Don't you ever think? I can't believe how careless you are. Or are you just stupid?"

"Sorry."

"It's a good thing one of us has brains, Robert! I had the girl believing my cell-phone was a gun," Nicole continued vehemently, patting her pocket again. "It worked like a dream, but you almost ruined everything, all with your loud, stupid voice. What's wrong with you?"

Erin ducked her head, on the verge of tears. The bulge wasn't a gun! She'd been tricked. And now it was too late to yell for help. Too late to run after the hikers. The only good thing about the entire frustrating experience was that now she knew the man's name — Robert.

"But it worked out okay," Robert responded, in an unwise attempt to defend himself. "Nothing happened. They kept going. So what's the big deal?"

Even Erin knew that this was the wrong thing to say to Nicole. She clapped her hands over her ears to block out the woman's infuriated retort the best she could. And besides, she needed to think. Now that she knew Nicole was unarmed, there might be another chance to escape. They might pass more hikers, and this time Erin would find a way to raise the alarm. How, would depend on how many there were. Three or more hikers could easily overpower Robert and Nicole, so she could just tell them she was being kidnapped. Even two hikers should cause the kidnappers enough trouble that she could escape.

And if they passed a single hiker, she could pretend to feel faint. That would make the hiker stop, and her kidnappers might be convinced she wasn't faking because she was awfully stressed. In fact, maybe she should even plan ahead and pretend to be a little unsteadier on her feet

38

than she actually felt. And after the single hiker stopped, what then? How would she let him or her know the situation?

Good question.

Somehow she had to figure out that part of the plan.

Talent, there they are. Finally we have caught them. I know you can see them too, with your sharp eyesight, even though night is coming on.

Come, let us move closer, as close as we can and still not be discovered. Let us see what opportunities for rescue arise. I promise you, we will attempt to rescue your girl this night.

When they started hiking again, Erin was careful to pretend to stumble every few minutes. Thankfully, the kidnappers seemed to accept that her unsteadiness was real. Siobhan wasn't the only one in their family who could act. Now if only some more hikers would come along.

The sunset slowly faded, the night crept nearer, and Erin felt her hope dying as the minutes slid past. By the time day had completed its transformation into night, she knew there was no point in pretending to stumble any longer. Everyone on the Burren would be camping now, settled into their tents or around their campfires.

They hiked on through the darkness for what felt like hours. The moon rose, then both the stars and moon disappeared as clouds covered the sky. Erin pulled her thin jacket tight around her body and kept trudging along behind Nicole. She was beginning to stumble for real and could feel blisters forming on her feet, when the woman finally let them stop.

Nicole lowered her backpack to the ground with a moan, stretched, then sat at the side of the green road. Erin slumped gratefully down beside her. She heard the woman unzipping her pack, and then Robert doing the same with his. What were they doing? If only the cloud cover would dissipate, she'd be able to see them by moonlight. A moment later, she heard the ripping of wrappers, then a delicious smell wafted toward her. Her stomach complained loudly. "Can I have some too?"

Nicole sighed. "You can give her some."

Erin heard a bit more rustling, then Robert pressed a piece of chocolate into her hand. "Thanks," she said, and stuffed the morsel into her mouth. The single bite was heavenly. She'd never tasted anything so wonderful! Probably because she was famished! Too soon — far, far too soon — it was gone. "Can I…"

"Time to go," said Nicole, interrupting her. She towered over Erin as she stood, a black form against the dark sky.

"Where are we going?" Erin tried again.

Once more, Nicole ignored her question. "Don't leave your wrappers for anyone to find," she said to Robert.

"Sorry," the man said. He always seemed to be apologizing to Nicole. His dark hulk bent to find his wrappers.

"Did you hear that?" Nicole asked abruptly. "Listen."

Erin held her breath. What had Nicole heard?

There! An almost inaudible clang, far, far away. Hope leapt to her heart, instantly rekindled, making her heartbeat roar in her ears. Had she heard right? Was it really horseshoe against stone? The noise was too far away to tell for sure, but that's what it sounded like. Was Talent coming to rescue her, just as she'd imagined? How wonderful!

"I don't hear nothing," said Robert, interrupting her thoughts.

"I'm sure I heard something, just for a second," said Nicole, puzzled.

"Goats," said Erin, trying to keep the jubilance from her voice. "It must be goats. There are wild herds on the Burren."

"Maybe," said Nicole, but she sounded doubtful.

"What else could it be?" asked Erin, hurriedly. Nicole didn't sound nearly convinced enough for her.

"I don't know," Nicole said, immediately suspicious. "You tell us. What else could it be?"

Erin clamped her mouth shut. All she was doing was making Nicole more wary of the sound. Now the woman was going to become even more guarded and watchful! Maybe if she pulled Nicole's own trick and simply ignored her question, the woman would drop the subject, thinking it was nothing.

But Nicole wasn't about to let it go. "What else could it be?" she asked again, even more insistently. "Do you know something you're not telling us?"

"What could she know? Let's get going. We're wasting time," said Robert from behind her.

With an exasperated sound, Nicole turned and began striding along the green road. Erin hurried after her. The last thing she wanted to do was incur the woman's wrath again – or remind her that the noise of iron on rock might mean something more important than goats.

The energy from the piece of chocolate didn't last long and soon Erin felt even more tired than before, but still, there was a bit of spring in her step, despite the blisters forming on her feet. She was positive Talent was out there somewhere, waiting for her to come to him, waiting to carry her to safety. She listened for any sound behind the sound of their hiking, beneath the sound of their breathing, between the occasional arguments between Robert and Nicole, as they trudged on and on and on. While she heard nothing more that might indicate he was there, still, she was sure he was near. She could feel him close by, as if he was somehow connected to her heart.

The clouds finally parted and moonlight splashed across the rocky Burren. Erin could see no living thing beneath the gentle glowing, and was relieved because she could tell that

Nicole was looking too. The woman's head moved back and forth as she scanned the landscape. Thank goodness, Talent had known to hide once the moon unveiled its light.

Erin gasped as one of her blisters suddenly burst, sending sharp jags of pain into her foot. Her boots were made for riding, not hiking. Surely, her kidnappers would see that she was limping now, and stop to rest a while. Then, if they slept, she could attempt an escape.

However, as the night wore on, Nicole showed no signs of stopping. Time lost meaning to Erin. The night seemed endless, eternal. She was sure they had trudged forever and would forever more. When Nicole led them from the green road, Erin risked pushing the button that lit up her watch to discover it was after three in the morning. The woman led them about a hundred yards to the right and stopped at an old ruin, a nondescript shepherd's shack.

Light speared from Nicole's flashlight as she searched the stone structure. Moments later, she emerged. "We'll stop here for a couple hours. I'm beat."

Robert slid his backpack from his back, too tired to comment.

Nicole straightened after spreading her sleeping bag out near the door. "You tie up the girl," she said to her partner.

"But…" Erin had to speak. She'd waited as long as she could.

"Shut up." Even Nicole's 'shut up' didn't carry much vigor anymore.

"But…"

"I said shut up."

"But I have to pee," she blurted out.

Nicole groaned. "Okay. Robert, tie her hands first. I don't want her running away from me in the dark."

Erin put her hand over her mouth to stop her satisfied

44

smile. The woman was so tired, she didn't realize she'd said Robert's name — again. And neither did he.

Robert pulled a coiled rope out of his pack. "Now don't struggle. This won't hurt." He pulled Erin's arms in front of her and wrapped the rough twine around her wrists. Erin flexed her muscles as he pulled the ropes tighter, and when Robert finished tying the knots, she lowered her arms and loosened her muscles. Her efforts had been successful. The ropes weren't too horribly tight. At the very worst, her circulation shouldn't be cut off, and at the best, if she were lucky, she would be able to squeeze out of her restraints after her captors were asleep.

Robert left a length of rope about two yards long, hanging from Erin's bonds, and Nicole grabbed it. "Come with me," she said, and tugged on the rope. Erin hurried after the woman as she led her around the side of the shepherd's stone shack and on a few yards further to a jumble of stones. "This is far enough," said Nicole. She stared off into the distance and tapped her foot as Erin fumbled awkwardly with her pants, and used the facilities.

On the way back to their camp, Erin studied the terrain in every direction. If she was going to escape tonight, she needed to know everything about the land that surrounded them. The Burren stones stretched like silver paving stones in every direction, open and visible to everyone who cared to look. If Nicole and Robert woke up when she was still close to the shack, they'd see her in the moonlight. She had to get far enough away that…

Suddenly, Erin's breath stopped short. She could see something moving over the Burren, something large and dark. Talent! It had to be! The form was far away, but was unmistakably a horse. And a rider.

"Hurry up." Nicole sounded impatient.

45

Erin ducked her head to follow the woman inside the shepherd's shack, her mind racing. The rider had to be her dad. He'd come with Talent. A thrill raced through her body and she felt lighter. Both of them had come to rescue her, and Nicole and Robert didn't have any idea they were there.

Now Erin just needed to wait for her kidnappers to fall asleep and her dad to burst in to save her. Or maybe she should stick to her original plan, and free herself from her bonds, then sneak away to where he and Talent waited. That would be far less dangerous for her dad. She would have to act fast, that's all.

Soon they will be asleep. They must be tired. They have traveled so far this night.

I hope your girl saw me, Talent. I think she did. If so, she should know to stay awake, and to be ready to run. We must get away without waking the kidnappers. Then we can be miles away before they discover she is gone.

Stop here and wait, my dear. I will go on alone. I know you want to come, but you must stay here, Talent. We can not risk alerting these horrid people with even the slightest brush of hoof against stone.

I will return as soon as I can. Watch for me, and for your girl!

Nicole was instantly irritated by what she saw inside the shack. Robert was lying close to the door, right in the spot she wanted for herself. When she turned on her flashlight, she felt even more annoyed. Crumbs and granola bar wrappers were scattered around him. He was such a dolt, eating most of tomorrow's food tonight. And then leaving the wrappers for the police again!

"You go sleep over there," she said to the girl, and pointed the flashlight beam to the back of the shack. It was stony back there, probably too rough and uncomfortable for the girl to actually sleep. She would be cold too, but Nicole didn't have an extra sleeping bag to give her, and she certainly wasn't going to give the girl her own. Besides, as soon as the kid was back with her family, she'd be pampered and cosseted beyond belief. A little discomfort right now would probably be good for her character.

Nicole followed her to the back of the shack. First, she checked the knot Robert had tied, and added a couple extra loops around the girl's wrists. Then she tied the end of the rope to the girl's ankles. She didn't want her running away in the middle of the night. Finally satisfied there'd be no trouble, she walked back toward the door.

The girl's needling voice followed her. "Is there a blanket for me?"

"No." Nicole quickly picked up Robert's wrappers, glared at his serenely sleeping face, and carried her sleeping bag outside.

Under the night sky, she felt the tension leave her shoulders. There was nothing to do now but rest. She rubbed her eyes. Yawned. She was so tired.

But there was still that strange noise she'd heard, hours before. Nicole frowned. Even more bothersome than the noise was the way the girl had reacted to it, as if she knew what it was and was purposefully keeping information from her captors: important information. The presence of a rescuer? Or someone the girl hoped was a rescuer? In the kid's own words, 'what else could it be?' And yet Nicole had seen no one on the Burren all night.

She sighed and moved silently away from the shack. A large stone sat a few yards from the doorway, and she lowered herself to the ground in front of it, leaned back, and pulled her sleeping bag over herself. From here, she could watch the doorway, while at the same time, be hard to spot, because she was sitting in the boulder's moon shadow. It was the perfect place to station a guard, and even though it was probably an unnecessary precaution, she felt better knowing she'd be ready — just in case someone came along.

Erin waited. She stared at the lump that was Robert, silhouetted against the moonlight streaming in the doorway, and searched for a clue that told her he wasn't sleeping. He didn't seem crafty enough to pretend he was asleep, but she couldn't be sure. And if he was actually watching her, she guessed he'd eventually give himself away, by either moving or making some sound of exasperation. Or he was simply sleeping. There was only one way to know for sure. She had to wait.

Erin huddled on her side, wrapped her tied arms around her knees in a vain attempt to keep warm, and pretended to sleep as she watched him possibly watch her. Some part of her mind caught the sick humor of the situation. Maybe they were both lying there in the dark, staring at each other, waiting for the other to show they weren't asleep.

When Robert finally did move, Erin's heart lurched in her chest. For a moment, she couldn't catch her breath. But all Robert did was roll onto his back. His mouth fell open and loud snores poured out, one after the other in a slow, gargley procession. They didn't sound like fake snores either. They were far too guttural for fake snores.

Erin wasted no more time. Moving as quietly as possible, she sat up, pulled her knees to her chest, and reached down to work on the ropes at her ankles. She was surprised that Nicole had tied her ankles without retying her hands behind her back in an attempt to stop her from loosening her own bonds. Obviously, both her kidnappers were too tired to think straight. Not that it would have worked even if Nicole had retied the ropes. Erin was sure she could've squeezed her body through the loop created by her arms — one of the benefits of being flexible.

Within a couple of minutes, her ankle ropes were untied. Erin moved on to her wrist ropes, grabbing at the first of Nicole's knots with her teeth. Nicole's two knots were easy to undo, though Erin's mouth and jaw were beginning to ache by the time she had them undone. Then she came to Robert's knot. The man was much stronger, and therefore his single knot was a lot tighter. Methodically, she worked it with her teeth, loosening it here, pulling it there. She could feel the minutes ticking by, each one an additional weight on her shoulders. She had to free herself and sneak out of the hut before her dad got too close, before he put himself in danger as well. He wouldn't know that Robert was lying just inside the door.

Though he'll hear Robert's snores, she reassured herself. The realization didn't comfort her much. Nicole could be anywhere outside, and all she had to do was yell to Robert to wake up.

Erin grimaced. She couldn't believe how much her teeth hurt. But she had to loosen the large knot. She was so close to freeing herself. She took a firm grip on the rough coil in just the right place and jerked back.

"Ow, ow, ow," she couldn't help but whisper and jammed her fist against her mouth. Her teeth felt like they were going to fall out of her head! But she'd felt the rope slip a tiny way through the knot. She was sure she had. She had to keep at it, no matter how much it hurt.

After the pain subsided a bit, she squeezed the knot

between her teeth again, and this time tugged gently. It was enough. Her last valiant effort had dramatically loosened the knot. A minute more and she was free of her bonds.

With her eyes locked on Robert's open-mouthed silhouette, she removed the baseball cap from her head, left it and the rope on the ground, and guardedly rose to her feet. She edged along the wall toward the door, her eyes probing for any movement, any sign that the man was waking up. At least she knew now he wasn't faking sleep. He would've jumped up the instant she was freed from the rope, if he was. No, Robert was resting peacefully. Now she just had to get outside without waking him — and she had to pray that Nicole wasn't outside staring at the doorway.

Closer, closer to the door. Her back scraped against the stone wall and she froze at the soft sound.

Move, she commanded herself, when Robert didn't stir. *Move.* In agonizing slow motion, she inched past Robert's head and then along the wall toward the door. Silently. Silently. One careful step after another.

Finally, she was beside the door. Her body trembled and her breath was shallow with fear. What would she find outside? Would she see Nicole in the darkness? Luckily, the moon was now bright in the night sky; otherwise there'd be no chance at all of locating the woman. Erin forced her gaze from Robert's gaping mouth and closed eyes, and slowly turned to face the doorway. She gripped the rock wall to steady herself, and leaned sideways to look out of the shack.

A form leaned sideways from the outside at exactly the same moment, like a mirror image. Erin almost screamed she was so shocked — but mercifully, her longing to escape

53

was stronger than her astonishment. She didn't scream. She didn't step backward onto Robert's prone form.

"Please, do not be frightened. I have come to help you." The voice was as soft as the night breeze, as delicate as wildflower petals. "Talent and I have come to help you escape. Now, follow me."

Nicole ran. As fast as she could, she ran. The creature was behind her, running as fast as she was. Without looking back, Nicole could sense its intent, could feel the tremble in the earth as it leapt along. It was a terrible thing, this creature pursuing her, but Nicole wasn't afraid. She'd had this dream before, and as always, she felt exultant, untouchable. There was no way the creature would ever catch her. She was running faster than she'd ever run before. The ground flew past beneath her fleetness. The wind streamed past her head, looking like blue and gray threads of light. She could hear the murmur of it in her ears.

But that wasn't right. The wind was supposed to whistle and shriek as it blew past, or at least it had every other time she'd had this dream. But this wind was soft. Serene. Peaceful.

Nicole shifted in her sleep. On the edge of her consciousness, she realized she was cold. Then she became aware that she'd fallen asleep in the most uncomfortable chair she'd ever encountered. Hard edges dug into her shoulder blades. A rocky spur was jabbing her in the back.

Groggily, she opened her eyes. Where was she? Why was she outside? Oh yes, they were on the Irish Burren.

She was carrying out her kidnapping plan. Robert was attempting to be of some use, if his actions could be called helping.

However one question wasn't answered. Who were the two people running away in the moonlight?

Erin ran after the strange girl, doing her best to ignore the stabs of pain from her blistered feet. She tried to get a glimpse of the girl's face, but all she could see clearly was her golden hair. It caught the moonlight like a glittering cape, swishing and swaying in front of her as they ran. Erin was sure she'd never seen the strange girl before — so how did the girl know she needed help? How had she found Talent? Even if she discovered him wandering the Burren, she wouldn't have known he was Erin's horse. She wouldn't have known his name.

"Wake up, Robert!" The cry ripped through the night behind them. "She's getting away!"

The older girl spun around and took Erin's wrist in a gentle hand. "You must go ahead. Talent waits for you in that direction." She pointed. "I will distract our pursuers."

"But how will you…" Erin gasped and took a quick step backward, jerking her wrist free. The moonlight was shining full on the girl's face now, making her skin glow pale and her eyes glisten — and her eyes were the color of amber!

"I am not the one to fear," the stranger said, insistently, urgently. She seemed desperate that Erin believe her.

And Erin did. "I… I'm sorry. You're right. I'm sorry," she stammered. "But be careful. Robert's very strong and Nicole is plain mean."

"Do not worry about me. You must get away. Now run!"

Her tawny eyes widened as she looked behind Erin. Nicole and Robert must be quickly coming closer.

"You should come with…"

"Run!"

Erin ran. As fast as she could, she ran. Moments later, light flashed behind her, light so bright that her own shadow became coal black in front of her and she had to slow down. She couldn't see where her feet might land — in a crack between the rocks? On a jagged stone? But thanks to the blonde girl, Erin knew it was probably okay that she was moving a bit slower. The kidnappers wouldn't be after her yet. The flare was so bright it had probably blinded them, for a few precious seconds at least. If only it could stop them long enough for her to get completely away.

But even if she escaped, what about her rescuer? What would happen to her? Wouldn't she be in even worse trouble than Erin had been? Wouldn't they be furious at the girl if Erin got away?

Slowly, the glare behind her faded and night resumed its soft moonlit glow. Erin ran faster as her eyes adjusted to the dimming light. She could hear sounds of a struggle behind her, and then, *horror*, footfalls thudding after her. The step was booted and heavy and very, very fast. Now she could hear labored breathing coming closer and closer. It had to be Robert!

A dark form pulled from the night in front of her, and she heard something else: the clanging of metal horseshoes on stone. Talent! She could see him now, cantering toward her in the moonlight. His hooves rang loudly on the natural pavement and his fiery mane flew about his high head and elegant neck like starlit silk. Erin had never seen anything so welcome, so beautiful, as her lovely Talent at that moment. Her hero! She had to get to his side before Robert caught her, well before, so she'd have time to climb into the big hunter's saddle.

But wait, she couldn't see a saddle in the moon's light. Had the strange girl untacked him? She could see no bridle on the finely etched head, and if the girl had taken the saddle off too, how was Erin going to get on the tall horse?

She needn't have worried about it. Five yards short of Talent, the hand came down on her shoulder. "No!" Erin shrieked. She tried to twist out of Robert's grasp, but there was no escape. Talent stopped and half-reared a few yards away, uncertain of what to do.

"Hold still now," Robert said, his voice infuriatingly calm and reasonable. "I'm not going to hurt you." His massive arm twisted around Erin's middle and lifted her off the ground, then he started carrying her back toward the hut. A moment or two later, Erin heard Talent following them.

"You have to let me go." She pounded on his arm to no avail. The man didn't even flinch. She would have to try something different, maybe even something she'd learned from Siobhan's psychiatric ramblings. Robert didn't seem like a cruel person. Maybe she could appeal to his better nature — before they reached Nicole and she was able to influence him.

"Robert, you know that kidnapping me is wrong, don't you?" Erin said breathlessly. He hesitated, but didn't answer her question. She continued. "It doesn't matter if you get money for me. You're not going to enjoy it. You'll feel too guilty. I can tell you're not a bad person."

No response. Time to try another tack. "Do you have a sister, Robert?" Erin felt him stiffen and his gait slow further. "How would you feel if someone kidnapped her?"

The man stopped. "But I can't let you go. What would Nicole say?"

"Why does it matter? You'll be doing the right thing."

"But she… You don't understand."

"I might," Erin said with as encouraging a voice as she could muster.

"Nicole *is* my sister. Our parents abandoned us when we were kids. She's the only family I have."

A disastrous setback. But still, her words had affected Robert; he obviously felt bad about kidnapping her. Maybe, there was still a small chance. "If I ride away on Talent, she never needs to know you let me go," Erin said quickly. "She'll just think I reached Tallie before you caught me and that I galloped away."

"But then I'd have to lie to her. I can't do that," Robert said firmly. The moment he started walking toward the shack again, Erin knew she'd lost. There was no way he was going to free her against Nicole's wishes. And there was no way she'd ever convince Nicole to let her go. That she knew for certain. She had one chance and one chance only of freedom — Talent.

"Tallie!" she screamed. "Tallie, help me!"

Immediately, the soft hoof beats in the dark turned to clanging metal as Talent trotted the few yards separating them. Robert whirled around so fast that Erin felt blood rush to her head. Talent's white-socked forelegs flashed in the moonlight as he reared above them.

Then Erin was flying backward, still firm in Robert's grip. "Tell it to go away," he shrilled, and for the first time since she'd met him, he sounded frightened. "Tell it to back off!"

Talent's front hooves met the earth, and he walked toward them, his head out straight and his ears flat against his skull. When he realized he couldn't reach Robert without hurting Erin, he reared again. He came down and sparks exploded toward the two humans. Then he went up again, whinnying and snorting.

"Go away!" Robert yelled again.

"Tallie," croaked Erin, feeling like a rag doll. "Help me!"

Talent stopped for a moment, as if confused by Erin's quiet tone, and Robert took the opportunity to back a few more yards toward the hut. But Talent wasn't about to let Erin go without a fight. He screamed, trotted toward them, and went up on his hind legs again. His front hooves churned the air above their heads.

Robert tried to back up again, but tripped — and Erin went flying through the air.

Her head struck stone and for a moment, she felt overwhelmed with a horrible immensity of pain.

Then everything went black.

The first thing Erin became aware of was pain radiating through her skull. She gasped with the agony of it. Wished she could black out again.

Then a soft muzzle touched her arm. A gentle whinny resonated around her.

"Tallie," she whispered. She opened her eyes and tried to sit up. Dizziness pushed her down onto the cold stone again. The horse whinnied, encouragingly, and bumped her with his nose. He was telling her to get up. And no wonder — she was on the ground. And it was the middle of the night. And her head felt like it was splitting open! What on earth was happening?

"Nicole! Nicole!" A man was shouting. "Come help me!"

Robert! Everything came back in a sudden, horrid rush. She was being kidnapped! Talent and a strange girl had come to save her. And unless she could get on her feet, right this moment, she would be recaptured!

"Tallie, help me," she whispered and reached up. Talent lowered his head, nickered softly. Erin clutched his mane. "Pull me up, buddy."

Slowly, Talent raised his head, pulling Erin to her knees, then his silky mane slipped through her rubbery fingers. She clutched at his forelegs for a moment, gasping with pain. She'd never known such agony! With one feeble arm she reached up and touched her head. A massive lump was forming on the right side of her skull. No wonder she felt so terrible!

But it didn't matter how awful she felt. She had to stand. She had to climb onto Talent's back! She had to escape! With a gallant effort, she pushed upward with her legs — then tipped sideways and fell heavily.

She could feel herself spiraling into the darkness again. "I can't, Tallie," she tried to whisper. She wasn't sure if she was actually speaking or just imagining it. Her ears were ringing too loudly to hear her own words. "But they're coming. You should run. Go get Dad. Bring him…"

Then darkness consumed her once again.

When Nicole heard the horse trot away into the night, she turned back to the pale girl. Let Robert take care of the kid. She wanted to figure this one out.

The teenager was such a dainty creature, almost otherworldly, and with all their surveillance and observation of Erin in the days before her kidnapping, they hadn't seen the girl once. She wasn't the sister, that was for sure, or one of Erin's friends that they'd seen. Was she a more distant relative? Or a stranger who noticed something didn't seem right out on the Burren and foolishly decided to be a hero?

She grabbed the blonde girl's shoulder and turned her over. The exposed face and arms were very pale, as if she rarely saw the sun. Her hair seemed drained of color. Nicole searched the ground around the still teenager. Where was the burnt out flare? That flare had been the oddest thing of all. It made the light seem to come from the girl herself, and not from anything she held in her hands.

And there was the fact she had collapsed, too, falling down for no reason whatsoever, after the flare finally died. It was all very confusing.

Nicole held her fingertips to the girl's throat. There was a slight flutter beneath the skin, a faint pulse. So she was alive. She hadn't dropped of a heart attack or anything like that.

Nicole scowled into the night. What were they going to do with her? It was bad enough that the kid knew Nicole's name. But now this one too, had seen her and could possibly identify her.

This job was becoming more and more complicated all the time!

The pain returned as Erin slowly became conscious again, but this time she felt a little more aware. She opened her eyes to see Robert approaching her, but no Talent and no Nicole. With a groan, she sat up and looked around. If only Talent had understood her and gone for more help. Her dad or the police would be best.

Robert grabbed her arm and gently hoisted her to her feet. "Are you okay?" he asked as he held her upright. "I'm sorry I dropped you."

"You threw me," Erin whispered.

"I'm sorry."

For the first time, Erin felt the same irritation that Nicole must feel with Robert – he was *always* apologizing, it seemed. As if the words made it okay that he'd flung her headfirst onto a rock. Even if it had been an accident. "You should have just let me go home," she added.

With a hand on her shoulder, Robert turned her back toward the shack. The ground seemed to lurch and dive beneath Erin's feet as she stumbled along, and her head pounded like it was filled with manic drummers. Nausea rose unwelcome inside her.

When they reached Nicole, Robert released her and Erin sank to her knees. Her rescuer was lying right in front of her, looking completely unconscious — or worse. Had Nicole harmed her?

"Uh, your... uh, you know," said Robert, his voice full of discomfort.

"What?" asked Nicole, and then interjected, "Hey, what's wrong with her?"

Erin looked up in time to see the woman leaning down to look more closely at her — and she noticed that Nicole looked different. Very different. Her bushy hair was no longer hiding her face. In fact, the mass of hair was completely gone. Nicole had been wearing a wig! Silently, Erin drank in the details of the woman's face. She had to remember everything about her later, so she could identify her to the police.

"I kind of threw her," Robert said, guiltily. "Sorry."

"You *kind of* threw her?" Nicole straightened, looked up into the man's eyes.

"Uh, you should... you lost something," Robert said. He reached out to touch her head but she slapped his hand away. Then her hand flew to her short blonde hair.

"Why didn't you say something sooner! You're such a..." She left the insult blank as she searched the ground.

"Sorry," muttered Robert.

Nicole found her wig and scooped up the tangled mess. "Now she knows what I look like!" The woman's voice was quickly becoming louder and the wig trembled in her hands like a furious beast.

"Sorry," Robert said again, but this time he didn't sound as apologetic. He sounded weary.

Nicole too, must have caught the inflection of his voice, but instead of making her calm down, it only fed her rage.

Erin groaned and put her hands over her ears as Nicole's voice raised higher, making her head hurt even worse. She looked at the unknown girl's face. Erin was sure she'd never seen this girl before in her life. She would've remembered her. She was such a striking-looking person, even though she looked a lot paler than she had fifteen minutes ago. Her hair was the color of gold then, and now it was white. And not even a shiny white at that. She looked as if the color had been sucked out of her, as if her energy and life force had been drained away.

Erin touched the girl's hand. The limp fingers were freezing cold. "Can you hear me?" she whispered in her quietest voice. There was no response. "Wake up," she whispered again. "Please, please wake up."

Without warning, Erin was grabbed from behind and hoisted into the air. This time Robert held her a little more gently as he carried her toward the hut. Nicole walked behind him, her voice sharp and needling as she continued their argument, her bushy wig once more restored to her head.

"We already might have hurt her. She looks so pale," said Robert.

Erin's heartbeat quickened. They were discussing the unknown teenager.

"So it won't hurt her any more to be tied up for a while."

"But what if no one finds her here?"

"You can't leave her tied up in the shack," interjected Erin, and the sound of her own voice sent pain radiating through her skull.

"You be quiet," snapped Nicole. "You have no say in this."

There was a long silence filled only with the sound of boots on stone. Then Robert spoke to Nicole. "Whatever you think is best," he said, and in that instant, Erin knew he was also telling her he had made his final choice. He was backing Nicole no matter what, even though he thought what she was doing was wrong. Robert was proving to be irritatingly loyal.

Talent. It is you. Though I am too weak to move, I can still sense you coming nearer. You have come back for me, my dear one.

Your tears fall, a blessed rain that restores life to my weak body. I am so grateful, Talent, more grateful than words can say. Please accept my undying love and gratitude.

We must go, but I am so weak still. I can not climb to your back.

Ah, you kneel before me to help me mount.

I am sorry that we were not successful in rescuing your girl, Talent. Please forgive me. But do not despair yet. I will try again, when my strength has returned. This is not over yet!

Nicole leaned against the doorway to the shepherd's shack, her silhouette dark against the outside light. "I can watch this one," she said to Robert. "You go get the blonde."

"Do you want me to tie her up for you?"

"No. She looks too sick to run."

Erin cried out when the beam from Nicole's flashlight touched her face, the light assaulting her eyes.

Robert raised his head, suddenly alert. "What's that?"

Nicole heard it too. "The horse is back," she said, and looked in the direction Erin knew the unconscious teenager awaited capture.

"What if it attacks me again?" Robert sounded afraid. Talent's attempt to rescue Erin had definitely unnerved him.

"Can't you take care of it?"

"It reared up and tried to hit me."

Nicole sighed. "Okay. Tie up the girl, and we'll both go."

"Thanks. Sorry." Robert wasted no time — and because he was in a hurry, he pulled the ropes too tight, jerked the knots too firm. Then he climbed to his feet and left the shack with Nicole.

Finally alone, Erin's tears began. Her would-be rescuer was just seconds away from being captured too! She struggled feebly against her ropes. If only there was something she could do, some way she could save the girl. But she could think of nothing. She was completely helpless to do anything, utterly useless. She couldn't even help herself, let alone the stranger. Seconds ticked past, then minutes.

"This isn't the place, I tell you!" Erin could hear Nicole's bellow all the way inside the hut. The woman was angry again. Why? Couldn't they find the girl? A flicker of hope rekindled.

Erin listened for Robert's response, but he was talking as calmly and reasonably as ever. Erin couldn't hear more than a distant murmur. But maybe, just maybe, the girl had escaped — maybe the sound of Talent's hooves was him taking her *away* from danger!

"I don't care what you think! She has to be here!"

Again, Robert's quieter voice; he was probably apologizing. Erin smiled wanly. All that time the girl must've been pretending to be unconscious. She couldn't have faked looking pale, so she must've felt sick. She just wasn't as incapacitated as she'd pretended to be. And then Talent had come and had taken her away to safety. What a great plan!

A minute later, Nicole stormed into the shack with Robert following meekly behind her. The man bent over Erin's bonds and picked at the knot, then gave up and pulled his knife from his pocket. "Hold still now," he said to Erin and started sawing on the ropes.

When Erin was free, Nicole approached her. She handed the girl the baseball cap she'd worn earlier. "Put this on," she said. "And as soon as we get far enough away from here, I'll take a look at your head."

Erin staggered toward the door. Outside the shack, both Nicole and Robert swiftly repacked their backpacks and reshouldered them. Then Nicole took a small object out of her pack's side pocket. "Shine the flashlight on the compass," she directed Robert.

73

"Are you sure we should do this? We won't be able to walk as fast. And she's sick."

"Once we're off the green road, no one will be able to track us, and besides, it's a more direct route across the Burren," said Nicole, briskly. "So, yes, I'm sure."

They think the girl's gone for help, Erin realized through her pain. The hatband, which had felt so loose before, was now tight around her head, making her heartbeat throb through her skull.

With Robert holding the light steady, Nicole adjusted the compass and slowly turned. "This way," she finally said, and without a backward glance, started out across the wild Burren.

In a daze, Erin followed her. Her head felt as if it was on fire, and she felt so muddled. She had to snap out of it! Unless she was aware, alert, attentive, there was no chance she'd escape, even if Talent and the girl came back. With or without additional rescuers, she needed to have all her wits about her. She had to be able to act!

I feel so helpless, Talent. So useless. My light did not intimidate the kidnappers. After their initial shock, the man simply ran around me to recapture your girl. There was nothing I could do then to save her.

We need a new plan, desperately. We will follow them, being careful to keep out of sight, but before too long, we must do something.

After the moon set, they slowed their pace, but didn't stop. Erin was doing her best to keep her eyes open, to look for chances to escape, to spot the strange girl and Talent or anyone else coming to rescue her, but every clear thought was a struggle. She kept lapsing into daydreams and irrelevant memories, like the day last week, when her friend Kayla came over and they groomed Talent until he glittered like a horse made of flame, and when they turned him out in his pasture, video camera ready to record him cavorting about and being beautiful, he headed straight for his favorite dusty spot for a roll. Except in her mind, the incident turned out a little differently than it had in real life. In her imagination, as Talent rolled happily in the dirt, she stretched out in the grass, closed her eyes, and slept.

Even the recurring daydream of Talent trotting toward her in the moonlight to rescue her, turned out strangely. After she'd miraculously climbed onto his strong back and Talent was carrying her away from her tormentors, she reclined across his silky withers, and fell into a deep slumber.

But it was no wonder her mind kept manipulating things. She was so tired! Unnaturally tired. As time went on and the desire to sleep became almost overpowering, she became sure her weariness was related to her head wound — which meant it was probably important that she stay awake! If she fell asleep, would she be able to wake up?

Even in her half aware state, she could tell that Robert was tired too. She kept hearing him stumble behind her. Nicole seemed to be in the best shape of all of them. She kept marching ahead, a dark silhouette striding straight through the night, stopping only to read her compass, and now and then to wait impatiently for Erin and Robert to catch up to her. Tapping her foot on the rocky ground. Hands on hips. Businesslike and cold. Surely Siobhan would have a psychological term to describe Nicole as well.

After they'd walked for what seemed forever, the ground became even rougher underfoot. They climbed up and then down, around bushes and through gullies in the dark. Whenever they came to a particularly jagged section, Nicole would shine her flashlight so the others could see. However, most of the time, Erin felt like she was walking blind through an obstacle course, with her head held together by the baseball cap. And all she wanted to do was lie down and sleep, for days, if possible.

When she felt she couldn't take another step, she noticed a finger of light stroke the sky to the east. A miniscule glimmer of hope sparkled in her mind. When daylight arrived, maybe someone would be there to rescue her: the girl and Talent, or even someone who might see her fainting routine. She glanced eagerly to the horizon, again and again, anticipating the light.

Her renewed hope was short-lived. She could tell long before the first rays lit the ground that she would not find her salvation with nearby hikers. The Burren here was wild and gullied. Brush clumped together on rough slopes, and sharp rock ridges ran through the shorter vegetation up and down the hills. No hiker would come to such a place, not when they had the green roads to travel. The girl and Talent wouldn't be able to track her here. No one would know where to find her.

"Stop," Nicole commanded sharply, and for a moment even the birds fell silent. Erin was more than happy to obey, and so it seemed was Robert. He plopped down on the ground and lay back, closing his eyes.

Nicole pulled some granola bars from her backpack, handed one to Erin, and opened one for herself. Erin pulled weakly at the wrapper, but soon gave up. For some strange reason, she wasn't hungry. But water, she wanted water. "Can I have a drink?"

Nicole handed her the canteen. "It's almost gone. Don't drink all of it."

Erin took a sip, then another, and almost vomited. What was wrong with her? She was incredibly thirsty, but the water was making her feel nauseous!

"Give it here,' the woman demanded. "And the granola bar too, if you're not going to eat it."

With wonderment, Erin looked down at her hand. Yes, there was a granola bar in her hand. Where had it come from? Dazed, she handed it to Nicole. The woman looked blurry, indistinct. Now she was leaning close. Erin blinked, and Nicole was gone. She looked around. There she was, standing beside Robert.

"Get up," she said to her brother. "We have to hurry. There's something wrong with her."

"What do you mean?" Robert opened his eyes.

"I think she has a concussion. We need to get there before she collapses," she said. "Unless you want to carry her, since it *is* your fault she's hurt."

Robert groaned as he climbed to his feet. "I'll carry her," he said.

"No," said Erin. She rose unsteadily to her feet. "I can walk." Stiffly, she started down the slope, lurched her way through the brush, and started up the other side of the gully.

78

"Wait. Have another drink," said Nicole, her words a command, not a request.

Erin stopped and the woman gave her the canteen. This time Erin was able to take three swallows before the nausea returned. She handed the canteen back to Nicole with a shaky grip, then struggled after the woman as best she could as they climbed the brushy gully slope.

Slowly, her nausea subsided. In fact, she was even feeling slightly stronger. Maybe the little bit of water had done her some good. She was feeling a bit more aware, a little less foggy. She looked up. Nicole was already at the top of the slope, looking down on Erin and Robert. "I see it!" she yelled. "Just a few yards farther!" Then she turned, walked onward, and disappeared from view.

At last, Erin reached the top of the rise. She stopped to look off into the distance. What had Nicole seen? Erin could see no houses, no people, no fences or animals, no roads. Nothing but blurry, shimmering rock, bright under the morning sun and edged in green.

But wait, there *was* something, in the distance, directly ahead of the woman. A stone rectangle — a wedge tomb: a burial chamber dating back to the Stone Age.

"Don't worry," Robert said behind her. "You won't be inside for long. And it's completely above ground. There's lots of light in there."

"You're going to put me in there?" Erin whimpered, finally understanding the obvious.

"We have to keep you somewhere. But we'll tell your dad where you are as soon as we get the money."

Erin felt tears come to her eyes.

"Please don't cry." Robert touched her shoulder in an effort to comfort her. When Erin shrugged his hand away, he muttered, "Sorry."

"You are *not* forgiven," slurred Erin, and walked toward the tomb, her throbbing head as high as she could hold it. After a moment, she heard Robert behind her, following meekly.

The tomb bobbed closer. And Robert was right: the structure did let in a lot of light. There were long cracks running between the massive stones.

And there was one more vastly appealing thing about the tomb. Once she was inside, Robert and Nicole would leave. And then even though she would be locked up, had an injured head, and felt exhausted and tired and sick, at least she would be away from her kidnappers.

And surely, surely, she could find some way to escape her prison.

At last they would get rid of this burden. From the looks of her, she wouldn't have made it much farther on her own feet. Nicole ground her teeth together. Robert injuring the girl like that had been a terrible stroke of luck.

Nicole stopped to search the rocky terrain. She knew it was unlikely she'd see anyone, and she was right. No one was there. She was just a bit on edge because of the escape attempt last night, that's all.

That strange teenager would almost be to the closest town by now, and then the search for the girl would begin. But they wouldn't find her, or not in time anyway. In just a few minutes, she would be in the wedge tomb, safely locked away from prying eyes, very effectively hidden — until she, Nicole, wanted the girl to be found.

Talent, stop! Someone is calling me away. I will return as soon as I can. I promise! Follow them, and keep at this distance. Be careful to not be seen, my love.

Bella Rio, it is I, Angelica. Hold steady, my dear, until I regain my strength. It always takes so much energy to transport to new places. I can feel your fear, your terror. And it is cold here. Wet. A current is sweeping around my legs.

Now I can see, and no wonder you are frightened! This is terrible! We must remove you from this dangerous place immediately! You and your stable mate, Duchess, are closed in your stalls, and there is water up to your knees! Floodwaters race down the barn aisle like a river! We must leave, now!

I will untie you, quickly. There, you are free, my fiery Bella Rio. And now you, my elegant Duchess. Come, let us leave this deathtrap. How the barn groans as we splash our way down the aisle. Hold now, while I slide the barn door completely open. There. We are free.

What a sight greets our eyes! Your stable yard is a river. Your owner's house is dark and appears empty. Did they just leave you here, without a thought? But no, you say, Duchess. They have been gone for almost two days, and the neighbors have been caring for you. They are the ones who have left you in this danger.

The water is quickly deepening. I can see it creeping up the side of the barn. And the barn is groaning under the pressure of the flood. Thank you, Bella Rio. Yes, I think I do want to get up on your strong dun back. Now, let us hurry toward the higher ground.

The wedge tomb was made of massive slabs of stone. A humungous single-slab stone roof sat squarely on top of the walls, which consisted of two slabs six feet long and four feet high along the sides, and one three feet wide on the end. At the other end, a massive stone lay on the ground, waiting to block Erin in.

Erin could hardly wait until they reached the stone structure, even though she knew she'd be locked away when she got there. Anything to rest. Anything to get away from Nicole and her shrill voice, Robert and his inane apologies. And then the tomb was right in front of her, the opening dark and welcome, the stone roof cool on her hands. Erin slowly lowered to her knees and crawled inside.

"Aren't you the eager one," Nicole said snidely.

"Just getting away from you," Erin answered.

Nicole laughed. "Okay, well let's get this over with. Robert, move the door stone into place."

Erin pulled the baseball cap from her head, sat back against the far wall, and hugged her knees to her chest. The shade inside the tomb felt wonderful on her light-sensitive eyes. In fact, in the shade, she could see much clearer. Some of the cracks between the massive stones even looked big enough for her to put a hand through.

After they're gone, I can stuff my jacket through one of the holes. If anyone passes, they'll see and be curious.

She tensed when the door stone thudded into place, making the entire tomb shudder with the impact, then put her hands over her ears to stop the sounds of heavy stones being dropped against the outside of the door slab to secure it in place.

Then, finally, blessed silence. Erin lowered her hands and closed her eyes. She was so sleepy.

"Hello. Is this Erin's father?" Nicole's voice was businesslike and efficient.

Erin jerked her head up, and the pain triggered by the sudden movement made her gasp. But Nicole was talking to her dad!

There was a short pause, and then Nicole spoke again. "Yes, we have her. We don't want to hurt her, so I'd suggest you cooperate."

Another short silence.

"That's good. Do you have the money?"

A longer pause this time.

"Okay," Nicole's voice was doubtful now. "I guess you can talk to her. I'll call you back in one minute." Nicole walked to the tomb. "Come here," she commanded Erin through one of the largest holes. "I'm going to hold the phone down so you can talk to your father. You tell him two things, and two things only — that you are fine and that you want to come home. Nothing else. *Nothing* else. Do you understand?"

Erin was silent. She didn't want to tell her dad she was fine. She wasn't fine at all.

"Do you understand?"

"I understand," Erin whispered. Painfully, she scooted closer to the corner of the tomb, and reached through the crack for the tiny cell phone.

"No, I'll hold it and you talk into it through the crack,"

Nicole instructed. Swiftly she dialed the phone again. "Here she is," she said, then held the phone down to the tomb.

"Can you hear me, Dad?" asked Erin.

"Erin, thank heavens you're alright!" Her dad's voice burst from the tiny phone, larger than life. Instantly, Erin was speechless. If only she could tell him where she was. If only she could climb through the phone to his end. She'd hug him so hard and never let him go! "Now you don't worry," her dad continued. "We're taking care of everything. You'll be home by tonight, okay? Okay, honey?" A pause. "Erin, are you there?" The fear in his voice was palpable.

"Dad?" she choked. "Dad, I'm scared." She couldn't stop the words from coming from her mouth, even though she knew Nicole would be angry. "And I don't feel… " Nicole jerked the phone away from the crack and Erin's words faded to a whisper, "…very good."

"Take the money to the abandoned castle on Muire Road before 8 o'clock tonight, and leave it inside the main chamber. After we collect it and are safely away, I'll phone to tell you where to find her."

She paused as Erin's dad spoke.

"No, you do what I say. I will call you when we're safely away. You have no say in this matter, not if you want to see your daughter again. And remember, no police." Erin watched through the crack as Nicole lowered the cell phone. She looked at Robert. "It's going to work. Now, we just need to go pick up our money," she said, her voice quietly jubilant. She gave Robert a rare smile. "As long as you remember which sea cave we use to get to the castle, of course."

Inside the tomb, Erin put her head in her hands. She felt so tired, so hopeless and sad and full of despair. She'd give anything to be home right now. Anything.

"I remember," said Robert, sounded defensive.

"Sorry. I'm just tired, that's all. Let's get going."

Erin peered out the thin crack between the door rock and the roof of the tomb. Her kidnappers were walking away to the east, toward the rising sun. She leaned her head against the cold stone. It felt so good against the heat in her head. Nicole had forgotten to look at her injury, Erin suddenly remembered, and then the thought disappeared in a wave of relief. Finally, she was safe from them. Trapped, yes, but her kidnappers were leaving. She waited for the sound of their footsteps to fade. At last, at long, long last, she was rid of them.

Now, with the scraps of energy and reason she had remaining, she could attempt her escape.

Hold, Duchess. Halt, Bella Rio!

Look ahead. The water is swift here. Deep. See how it swirls and eddies over the section just before us?

You want to go forward, Bella Rio? But it is too dangerous!

Yes, I trust you.

If you say this is the way to go, if you say it is safe here, I believe you. But tread cautiously, Bella Rio. Step with care, noble Duchess.

Ah, the water here is indeed swift, but it is shallow. We are crossing the flooding river — on a bridge hidden beneath the muddy water. But you, my dears, you knew this was the right way.

And we are now beyond the worse rapids. Let us continue onward. The water is still all around us. Still, it is rising.

Erin pressed her back to the slab the kidnappers had put in place, lodged her heels in a crack in the earth, and pushed, tentatively at first, then harder and harder, until she was straining with all her strength. But the entrance stone stood solid, refusing to budge even a fraction of an inch. With her breath coming in gasps, Erin pushed again, this time until her face felt burning hot and sweat prickled her body. Harder, harder she pushed, and then harder still, harder than she thought possible.

"Sorry." The word came from over her shoulder and Erin yelped. She scrambled, wild-eyed, away from the stone. Robert was looking at her through the crack. "Nicole asked me to come back," he said.

"Hurry up," Nicole called from a distance. "We haven't got all day."

Robert tried to put his hand in through the hole, but it was too big to fit easily. "We need the hat back," he said.

Erin swept the hat from the ground, leaned forward to stuff it through the hole, and jerked back. She didn't want it anyway. She didn't want anything that belonged to Robert or Nicole — except maybe some water.

"Can I have a drink?" she asked.

Robert took the hat, and straightened. She could hear him opening his pack, and assumed he was putting the hat away. Then he bent down to the crack again, a granola bar

in his hand. He pushed it through the hole. "It's my last one."

"Thanks," whispered Erin.

Then Robert was holding out his canteen. Trying to push it through the hole. It was too big.

"Put your hands through the hole."

Erin did.

"Robert, what are you doing?" Nicole sounded exasperated.

"Hurry," the man muttered. "Or she'll get mad again."

Erin cupped her hands and he poured water into them. She pulled her hands back inside the tomb and slurped up the water. Pushed her hands out for more. He refilled her cupped hands.

"Like I say, don't worry," he said, trying to reassure her. "You're going to be fine. Just go to sleep for a while and you'll feel better." He stood. "Coming. Sorry," he called to his sister.

As Erin watched him hurry away, pity rose up inside of her. If anyone was ever in the wrong occupation, it was Robert. How did he ever let Nicole talk him into doing this?

The man had reached his sister now, and the two of them were walking away, side by side, Robert with his lumbering stride, and Nicole with a free, self-confident swing to her arms.

And even though she was alone, injured, and locked in a tomb, Erin wasn't one bit sorry to see them go.

Nicole glanced back at the tomb, a smile of satisfaction on her face. This place was so remote, she was sure no one would find the girl until they told them where she was. It was the perfect hiding place, basically confirming their success in collecting the money.

Soon she would be lying on a beach, soaking up the sun and the tropical atmosphere with a drink in her hand. This entire misadventure would be like a bad dream that happened long ago, not even worth an afterthought.

And how she was going to love being rich again! She'd run out of money from her last kidnap victim almost three months ago, and there were so many things she wanted to buy. A fancy car, first of all. A nice silver one. And maybe a villa somewhere — but on second thought, no villas. It would be more fun to travel the world this time. It would be expensive, especially since she'd go first class, but that was okay. She just needed to remember to plan her next kidnapping a bit sooner, before she actually ran out of money.

Robert's beat up little car was right where they left it, on the stony track she was sure no one traveled more than two or three times a year. She'd researched that as well.

Now, they would drive to that dingy little hotel they'd selected and she would check in, paying cash for her room so she couldn't be tracked by her credit card. The first thing she planned to do was have a bath. She felt so disgustingly dirty, filthy enough to even forego her planned nap for a few minutes. The nap would be the second thing she'd do, a nice long one. She was so tired! And she should be undisturbed as she slept. Robert was going to check into a different room, an hour or so after she did, so the desk clerk wouldn't know there was a connection between them. Just another safety precaution.

And after her long nap, she would wake refreshed, meet with her brother, and away they'd drive to collect their hard-earned money. Once again, she would be living the rich life she was meant to live.

Bella Rio, listen.

You say you recognize the sound coming from around the corner? It is your people's truck! They are coming to save you! How wonderful!

I will bid you adieu, my dear Duchess and Bella Rio. I will let you greet your people alone. They will be relieved to see you well. Goodbye, my loves.

And yet, I will linger for just a moment. I will watch their reunion from behind this tree, to make sure all is well.

The truck splashes around the corner of the flooded road and stops. A man opens the door and jumps out, not caring that his clothes are becoming wet. A woman and young boy climb out the other side of the truck, the boy piggybacking on his mother's back. He has tears on his face, but he is smiling, one of the biggest smiles I have ever seen!

The man has reached Duchess now. He puts his arms around her sleek black neck and hugs her. How lovely to see such care, such regard for these, my equine friends.

I must return to Talent now. No more lingering. Bella Rio and Duchess are safe. I am free to go.

Erin waited for five long minutes before she tried to escape again. She needed to concentrate, to re-evaluate her situation. Obviously, the door stone her kidnappers had put in place was not going to move, at least with the amount of power she could exert against it.

She could see there was no hope of moving the side wall rocks either. They were far bigger than the slab Robert and Nicole had put in front of the door, and besides, the massive stone that was the roof was resting on top of them, holding them into place. She closed her eyes and leaned against the door stone. Immediately, she felt she was spiraling down a dark tunnel, and jerked her head up, opening her eyes. She had to stay awake! She had to think!

The way she saw it, she had three options left: find some other way to move the door stone, push away the other end rock wall, or dig her way out. Erin forced her eyes to focus, and searched the ground. There was only one narrow strip of earth in the tomb, lying between the two slate slabs that made up the rest of the floor. She shuddered. Did that mean there were two people buried in the tomb, perhaps thousands of years ago?

No, don't think about that. Not now. It's too awful. The dirt seam was almost a foot wide. If she was able to dig down deep enough, chipping away and removing the dirt from where the seam ran under the wall, she might be able to squeeze her way out — assuming the seam was the same width deeper down. Erin didn't have a lot of hope that it was. The wildflowers that grew in the sliver of soil were awfully small. It could be because the tomb kept the rain off them, but it was also possible that the soil was so shallow that they didn't have the nutrients to grow very big.

There was only one way to find out. Erin took a small, sharp rock in her hand and weakly scraped away the earth in one barren spot. It didn't take her long to realize that her second guess was right. Just two inches down, the seam of dirt turned into rock. Erin choked back her disappointment. There would be no digging her way out. But she couldn't give up hope yet. There might still be other things she could try. She just wished she felt stronger. Her head felt like a huge, unbalanced ball on her shoulders, and she was shivery and hot and sluggish and sleepy, all at the same time.

After another look through the cracks to confirm that Nicole and Robert were still gone, Erin crept to the opposite end of the tomb. This time she lay with her back on the cold ground, pressed her boots flat against the smaller wall stone, and pushed. It was like pushing against a solid mass. She wouldn't be moving this rock either.

She tried to sit up, to move on to the next plan — whatever that was — but dizziness forced her down again. She lay for a minute, head spinning and thoughts tumbling around each other.

Moving the door stone is probably my best bet, she decided sleepily. *Maybe there's some other way I can push it out of the way.*

Still lying on her back, she painfully turned her head both ways to scan the interior of her prison. There was no wood inside the tomb, but one of the rocks was longer and thinner than the others. Was it long enough to use as a pry bar?

Would the end of it even fit through the largest crack? And all that was assuming she was strong enough to lift it into place. It looked very heavy.

Erin closed her eyes and allowed her warm breath to trickle out through her nose. She'd try to pry the door open in a few minutes, after a quick rest. Small pebbles dug into her back, but she didn't have the energy to brush them out of the way, or even to adjust her position. She felt as if a heavy blanket was slowly settling over her, pressing her down and flattening her out on the stone. Her pain became distant, fuzzy.

Erin knew she should open her eyes, knew she should sit up, even if it hurt, but she couldn't quite muster the will. She no longer had the power to fight the unnatural sleep — and so it closed around her, firm and unrelenting, claiming her as its own.

A voice sounded in her mind, sharp and strident. Erin couldn't understand what it was saying. It seemed too far away. Too remote. But even then, she could tell the voice was unpleasant.

"Wake up!" There it was again, louder. Siobhan!

"Go away," Erin muttered. She liked oblivion. She liked not being aware. It was so much less painful. And what right did Siobhan have to tell her what to do anyway?

"Wake up, Erin. Don't be such a loser!" Erin opened her eyes. It had to be her imagination. Her stepsister didn't know where she was. Slowly, her eyes shut again.

"You're just a lazy brat! I think you're…" Erin's eyes popped open again, and Siobhan's voice faded away. So it *was* her imagination. But why was she imagining Siobhan's voice?

Probably because she's the most irritating person I know. Erin grimaced. No other imagined voice could make her wake up — unless it was Robert's or Nicole's. And Siobhan was infinitely preferable to them!

Erin bit her lip as she pushed herself up onto her elbows. Fresh tears gushed from her eyes. Her head hurt so much! She held still for what seemed forever, waiting for the pain to subside, and when it didn't, she pushed herself to a sitting position anyway. She sat hunched over, her head in her hands, and concentrated on staying awake. Seconds dragged past, then minutes.

A clang came from outside the crypt. Had her kidnappers returned? Or was it her imagination again? With agonizing movements, Erin crawled to the crack between the stone roof and the entrance stone to see the most amazing, welcomed sight she'd ever seen! She closed her eyes, and reopened them, then rubbed away the tears that clung there.

Please make this not be my imagination, she prayed. *Please make it be real!*

With her blurred vision, she could see Talent just a few yards from the tomb, picking his way through the rocks toward her! And he wasn't alone. Someone was on his back. The chestnut hunter glistened in the morning sun and Erin was almost blinded by his glory. Her rescuers — if they were real.

"In here!" she said, loudly, and flinched when the sound of her own voice seared her mind with burning pain.

She was infinitely relieved when Talent whinnied in response and the girl on his back waved to acknowledge Erin's shout. They had to be real! However, as the horse and rider came closer, Erin could see that this girl was no one she'd seen before. Though she looked similar to the teenager who'd tried to rescue her last night, this girl's hair billowed like orange-red silk about her head. Another stranger!

Talent reached the tomb, stopped, and pawed the ground. Snorted. The stranger slid from his strong back. Erin blinked a few times, confused. Maybe she *was* hallucinating. The girl's hair had just shimmered into an iridescent gold.

The girl bent to look through the crack at Erin. "Are you all right? You look so pale."

Erin scrutinized the girl. "Uh, your hair. It looked, uh, different a minute ago."

"Oh that," the girl said dismissively and rolled her tawny eyes. "It just does that."

100

"What?"

"It changes color to match the horse I am riding."

Erin had never heard anything so bizarre. "That's too weird," she said, her words slurring.

The girl's forehead creased with worry.

"Are you okay?" Erin asked, wanting to forget her own weaknesses. "You looked sick last night."

"Yes, I am *okay*," the girl responded, the worried expression still firmly entrenched on her face. "But you are not well."

Erin almost said, "You talk funny," but at the last moment was able to stop the words from escaping her mouth. What was wrong with her? She didn't want to be rude to her rescuer. It was true the words the older girl used were quaint and old fashioned, but still. "What's your name?" she asked instead.

"My name is Angelica. What is your name?"

"Erin. Thanks for rescuing me." She was half aware that she was speaking far slower then she normally did. Or maybe it only seemed that way. Maybe she wasn't speaking at all and was just dreaming all this. "And thanks for trying last night, too." And now her own words were starting to echo around in her head. She put her head in her hands and closed her eyes.

"Just sit still, Erin. I will move the rocks before the door stone." Erin heard her roll the rocks sitting in front of the door slab away from the wedge tomb. Each sound of stone grating against stone made her flinch. Finally, the noises stopped and Erin looked up. The girl — what was her name again? Erin couldn't remember — was looking in through one of the cracks at her. "Can you push in the same spot that I pull?" the girl asked. "Do not try if it will hurt you further."

"No, I can help," Erin said, her voice weak but determined.

The pale girl reached inside the tomb, and Erin noticed that her hands were small, almost like a child's. Both fit through the crack at the top of the door stone, whereas even one of Robert's wouldn't fit. Somehow she thought that funny, and giggled.

The girl gripped the edge of the door rock and strained backward. Erin collected herself in time to push on the rock just below the tiny hands, and almost fell forward when the rock shifted outward. Light spilled in through the opening and speared her eyes. She cried out and jammed them shut.

"The opening is still too small for you to escape. Hold still. I will do the rest," the girl said from somewhere far away.

"I can help," Erin whispered and with her eyes still shut, put her hands against the stone. Pushed. And suddenly the door rock wasn't there anymore. She heard it thud against the ground and felt the sun on her face, then the girl's cool hand on her arm.

"Come." The word was so soothing. So musical. "Let me help you out."

Gladly, Erin crawled toward the pressure on her arm. Even in her half aware state, she noticed the surprising strength in the girl's hands. And mysteriously, she was feeling a little better now. Maybe it was safe to open her eyes. She peered through thin slits. The brightness of the day didn't hurt her eyes so much this time. With relief, she opened them wider. The girl — her name was Angelica, Erin remembered now — was kneeling beside her.

"I have to get home," Erin said, and tried to stand. A dark whirlwind of dizziness enveloped her and she slumped back to the ground.

"Just lie down on this rock and rest for another minute or two," said Angelica. "The sun has warmed it a little. Now close your eyes and relax. Soon you will feel better and then we will go get you some water." Her hands joined at the top of Erin's head.

"I'm okay, really," Erin murmured, but she gratefully lay back as Angelica suggested. She closed her eyes. Breathed slowly, evenly. She was free! Thanks to Talent and Angelica. And she was feeling so wonderful now, so relaxed and peaceful. The sun-kissed rock felt comfortable and welcoming, and her injury wasn't hurting nearly as much now. In fact, her head even felt warm and tingly where Angelica's hands rested, and she wondered how that could be when the girl's hands had felt so cool before. She heard Talent's shoes ring on stone as he moved to stand closer to her. When he nuzzled her hand, she opened her eyes, smiled up at him, and lifted her arm to stroke his face. "I'm okay, Tallie," she said, weakly. "Thank you, too. I owe you both so much."

"Stay still for another minute or two," Angelica suggested. "And close your eyes. Relax."

Erin sighed and closed her eyes. Every muscle in her body felt as if it was melting into tranquil goo. "You're not from around here?" she managed to ask.

"I am from another place."

"I thought so. Your accent, I mean." Erin wondered why she hadn't seen it before. If Angelica was a foreigner, it totally explained why her words sounded so old-fashioned and perfect. "I'm glad you decided to come here for your holiday," she said, lazily. "If you hadn't come ..." She couldn't finish the sentence. It was too unpleasant to think about and she didn't want to disturb the peace. She drew in another long, contented breath. Yes, she was definitely feeling much better now. Her wound didn't hurt at all anymore, even though Angelica was almost touching it.

Her headache was completely gone. Her blisters weren't stinging, and her tired body felt as if it was floating in a cloud, a perfect, painless cloud. She never wanted it to end. Never wanted to move.

But she had to. She had to let her dad know she was free. He was probably beside himself with anxiety. And now there was no reason for him to give the kidnappers any money or for him to put himself in danger by going to the dilapidated castle. She sat up.

"You are feeling better now." It was a statement, not a question.

"So much better. It's amazing. All I needed was to get out in the sun, and to rest a bit. I thought it was more serious."

"You need water still. Come. Let us go to the stream I mentioned. We will ride together."

Oh Talent, I am so relieved we got here when we did. Your girl was on the verge of delirium, because of her exhaustion and that nasty head wound. I am so thankful we arrived in time.

But what about their next victim? Will the next child taken have a horse who will call me to help? Probably not. I know you feel we should put a stop to the activities of these unkind people while we can. I agree, we should try.

But what do we do? We need a plan.

Erin bent over the bubbling stream and scooped water to
her mouth. She'd never tasted water so pure and delicious!
It was cool, and refreshing, and almost sweet in her mouth.
She scooped up handful after handful, then when that wasn't
fast enough, lay down on her stomach and drank directly
from the rushing brook. After a moment, Talent decided he
was thirsty too, and plunged his muzzle into the clear water
beside her.

Erin ducked her head into the water to wash her face, and
it was only when she rose up, dripping with cold water, that
she thought it odd that her head didn't hurt at all. In fact,
there was no longer even a bump on the side of her head.
Had Angelica healed her?

Erin looked at the older girl sitting on the bank with an
amazed expression. Who was she, really? She had so many
questions for her. Like how did she know Talent? And how
did she know Erin was in trouble? Why had her hair turned
white last night, and how had she been healed herself?

But on second thought, Erin considered, *maybe I don't
want to know the answers. Angelica's explanations might
make everything seem less magical — I mean, there must be
a logical reason behind everything that's happened — and I
like to think that magic is involved.*

Cold water was dripping from her hair and onto her
shoulders, and she shook her head to get rid of the excess

water. When Talent snorted and raised his head to avoid getting wet, she laughed apologetically and climbed to her feet. "I'm sorry, Tallie," she said and stroked his shoulder. The horse took a few more sips, and when he finished drinking, Erin gave him a hug. "You are the most wonderful horse in the world, Tallie," she murmured into his red mane. "Thank you again, and again, and a thousand, million times more, too." The horse felt so strong and smooth beneath her hands, like silk covered sinew. She breathed in his wonderful scent, deeper, deeper, and could feel his strength infusing her too, bolstering her energy.

Finally, she turned to Angelica. "I need to let Dad know I'm okay, and it'll take too long to ride home first. I don't want him to worry too much or to give the kidnappers any money. We need to find a payphone."

"Yes, that is a good idea," said Angelica. She linked her hands together and Erin used them as a stirrup to climb onto Talent's back, then the older girl leapt up lightly behind. "In which direction do we travel to reach the nearest telephone?"

"That way. There's a little town there." Erin pointed to the west. As if he'd understood her, Talent turned away from the rising sun and picked his way through the rocks. She leaned over and stroked his shoulder. "Good boy," she whispered, and then straightened. "We need to be careful to find a payphone on a quiet street though, because it's the closest town to where the kidnappers are picking up the money." She shuddered. "And I don't want to ever see them again."

"So you know where your kidnappers plan to pick up the money?" There was a hopeful lilt in Angelica's voice.

"I heard them talking. Dad's supposed to leave the money in the old castle ruins on Muire Road. It's a long way from any other houses, and near the ocean. They told him to drop it off, and that after they had the money they'd phone to tell him where I was." She closed her eyes and let the safe sound of twittering birds fill the silence. "I'd still be in the tomb if it wasn't for you and Tallie. I'd still be sick. You and Tallie totally rescued me." She opened her eyes again to the glorious dawn light. The sun was climbing higher behind them and the Burren glistened gray and vibrant green around them.

Angelica patted Erin's arm. "I did not do anything that you would not have done for me, or for anyone else in trouble," she replied.

A small smile touched Erin's face. What Angelica said was true. If she'd seen someone in a bad situation on the Burren, she would've done what she could to help. "You know, Angelica, there is someone else in trouble, or there will be." Erin's voice was slow, thoughtful. "Someone that we can help."

"You are thinking of the next victim of the kidnappers. Am I right?"

"Yes. When they don't get any money from Dad, they might just kidnap some other kid, and I don't want anyone else to go through what I did." Her voice became harder as she continued. "And Nicole especially needs to go to jail for what they did to me. Robert's not as bad. At least, he *tries* to be nice. But Nicole is awful." Her face was getting hot, and for a moment, she struggled to control her anger. Not that her kidnappers didn't deserve her rage. They certainly did! But she didn't want them manipulating her emotions any more. It would be far more satisfying to simply get even with them.

"You sound as if you have an idea," observed Angelica. "Do you know how we can capture them?"

"Yes. When I phone my dad, I'll tell him to go ahead and

take some fake money to the castle. As long as he phones the police first, he should be safe. They can hide around the castle — there are lots of ruins there — and catch the kidnappers when they come to get the money."

"That is an excellent plan," said Angelica. "The police can capture these criminals. And all that remains for you to do is to ride home after you telephone your father."

An abrupt and shocking tremor of fear ran through Erin's body. She was afraid to ride across the Burren! She wanted her dad to come get her. She wouldn't feel safe again until she was with him. In fact, she wondered if she ever wanted to leave home again. She could always ride Talent in the riding ring and on her own property. She could ask the teachers to send her schoolwork home. She'd invite her friends to her house to visit, and her dad could be there to protect her. He could do his work from home.

But Angelica was right. She had to be tough, for just a few hours more. If her kidnappers saw her in her dad's car, or saw him driving about, or noticed anything suspicious at all, they'd know not to go to the castle that night.

So she had to ride across the Burren one last time. With Talent and Angelica with her, she just might be able to muster the courage.

Nicole yawned and stretched on the hotel bed. Her nap hadn't been nearly long enough. She was still tired.

She glanced at her watch. Six more hours. It was still so early. Why had she awakened? She still had six agonizingly long hours to wait. Six hours until she was rich. Six hours to sit in a cheap hotel room and stare at the ceiling — unless she could get back to sleep. She rolled over, closed her eyes.

A gentle knock sounded through the small room. Instantly, Nicole was off the bed and hurrying toward the door. She peered through the peephole.

What was Robert doing here, so brazenly going against their plan? He was supposed to be waiting in his own room. They were supposed to act like they'd never met. And yet he was standing in broad daylight, outside her hotel room, and knocking on her door!

He knocked again, louder.

"Hold on," she said before he started calling her name too. She opened the door and stood back to let him enter.

"Sorry, Nicole. I was just bored," he said, as if that made it okay to disturb her rest.

With barely controlled anger, she closed the door behind him. "Well, what can I do about it?" she asked, her voice reed thin.

"We can watch TV together."

Nicole felt her face grow hot. How she longed to yell at him! But she couldn't even argue. If they started quarrelling, her voice would get too loud and someone would hear. And that was all they needed — someone to notice them together. Someone to remember them. There was only one thing she could do. Control her anger.

Robert took her silence as agreement and grabbed the remote control. The TV sound blared into the tiny room. Without turning down the volume, he flipped channels until he came to a car chase.

Nicole started pacing back and forth in the small space.

"Hey, you keep getting in the way," Robert protested, the second time she strode past the TV.

Nicole ignored him. She was running a calming chant through her head, the only thing that could possibly keep her from screeching at him right now.

Only six more hours, only six more hours, only six more hours, only six...

"Dad!"

It was all she could get out before he started shouting into the phone. "Erin! Are you okay? Have they hurt you? If they have, I'll…"

"Dad, don't worry. I'm okay. I got away."

"You what? You escaped!" His laugh was unnaturally loud. "Trust my wonderful, brilliant daughter to get the best of those kidnappers! Where are you? I'm coming to get you, right now!"

Erin paused. This was going to be the tricky part. "Dad, I don't want you to come get me. Now wait, just hear why before you disagree, okay?"

"It won't do any good."

"But Dad, you have to do what I ask. The kidnappers will just kidnap someone else if they're not caught. I want you to call the police to help you and take a duffle bag of newspapers, or something besides money, to the castle tonight. Then when the kidnappers come, you and the police catch them, okay?"

"That's a good plan, Erin, but I'm still going to come pick you up."

"But Dad, they might have someone watching the house," she said. "Or they might see you driving, or even me in the car with you. They won't go to the castle at all then, and the next kid they take might not escape."

"But I can't just leave you…." His voice was hushed.

"Yes, you can. And besides, I'm not alone. Tallie's with me. I'll ride him home and this time I *won't* get off him. I promise."

"Talent? He's with you? But how?" Her dad sounded confused. "He went to rescue you? All by himself?"

Erin looked at Angelica standing beside her horse. She'd already promised the girl she wouldn't tell anyone about her. She hated lying to her dad, but after everything Angelica had done for her, how could she refuse her only request? "I guess so," she replied.

"Are you sure you're all right, Erin?" The strain in his voice was palpable. "Even if I shouldn't come, I'll phone the police to pick you up."

"No, don't, Dad. I'm fine, really," she said, quickly. The last thing she wanted was a stranger to come pick her up. She'd much rather ride across the wild Burren. At least then she would be with Talent and Angelica, two individuals she trusted completely. "I'll see you tonight after you catch the kidnappers, okay? I'll ride to the old stonecutter's cottages just to be sure the kidnappers don't see me, and wait for you there. And then I'll tell you everything that's happened." *Or almost everything,* she amended in her mind.

"Erin, you have to tell me where you are."

"I can't, Dad. I'm sorry." Emotion was starting to choke her voice. How she hated doing this to him, but she really couldn't bear the thought of getting in a car with a stranger, not even a police officer. And her Dad couldn't come. He had to act completely as if he still thought she was kidnapped. "I'll start back now, Dad. I'll see you tonight. Bye."

She replaced the telephone receiver before he could respond. They needed to start back right away, if they were

114

going to make it to the stonecutter's cottages in time. It had taken hours to find a suitable payphone. However, it had been worth it. Now her dad knew that she was safe and to call the police. Together, they would capture her kidnappers. After all she'd been through, at least Nicole and Robert would be going to jail.

It was the longest afternoon of Nicole's life. Every minute stretched to feel like an hour, every hour a week. It was as if the universe was conspiring to make her go insane with frustration. Robert was driving her crazy, playing one stupid, senseless show after another on the TV.

It was a terrible atmosphere for intense thought, and Nicole really needed to think. Though Robert didn't know it yet, they had a problem. The girl knew her name, might even know Robert's name, and because Nicole's wig had fallen off, the girl could identify her. No matter which way she looked at it, there seemed only one solution: not tell the parents where their daughter was. Leave her in the tomb.

Four hours until they were to go pick up the money, and Nicole had already turned the problem over in her mind a hundred times. But she could think of no alternate solution.

Three more hours. She'd have to lie to Robert if she did. He'd never go along with it. He even liked the kid.

Two more hours, and she still hadn't answered the question. And there was one other thing to consider: there was still a chance the girl might die anyway. She'd obviously had a concussion when they left her there.

One more hour. If they left her, it would destroy Nicole's perfect record. Up to this point, she'd never harmed a single kid in the kidnappings she'd planned.

116

What should she do?

Finally, it was time to go. Nicole carried her backpack into the bathroom and pulled out her all-black clothes. Though the money would probably be waiting for them, unprotected — after all, she'd warned the girl's father about calling the police, and they were planning to approach through the secret underground tunnel — one couldn't be too careful.

She took a final look at herself in the mirror and smiled at the color in her cheeks. Now that it was almost time, she was feeling excited. The payoff for all her hard work had finally arrived. And she would decide what to do about the girl after they had the money.

Soon, very soon, she'd have everything she deserved.

The afternoon ride across the Burren had been lovely. The day was glorious and the thud of Talent's shod hooves along the green road was comforting. The birdsong and leaves rustling in the breeze were like music.

Erin was surprised she was able to relax after her harrowing experiences with the kidnappers and knew it was all because of Angelica. Every time she imagined one of the kidnappers looming out of a gully, or from behind a bush, or sneaking up behind her, Angelica would say something funny or bring up an interesting topic.

Erin asked Angelica a couple of questions about her life, and at first, she thought it odd that the older girl always seemed to turn the topic back to Erin, or to horses, or to the country they were traveling through. However, after a while, she accepted that Angelica didn't really want to talk about herself. Still, she was incredibly interesting to talk to. In fact, Erin couldn't remember the last time she'd felt so entertained.

Time flew past and Erin was surprised when she first noticed the sun was low on the horizon. She patted Talent on his neck. Their steady pace had been good. They were only an hour away from home and would arrive at the stonecutter's cottages just before her dad. Perfect timing. In fact, it was probably about time for her dad to arrive at the castle ruins.

Holding her breath, Erin looked to her right, something she hadn't realized she'd been avoiding until that moment. Yes, there it was — the castle. Miles away, silhouetted against the sea. She inhaled sharply.

"Do try not to worry," said Angelica. "I am sure your father will be fine. The police will make sure he is safe."

"I know." Erin jerked her gaze from the ruins and looked down at Talent's red mane. She started to tremble, and the horse stopped short, looked back at her, and nickered. "It's not just that. It's ... it's... hard to explain."

"I am listening." Angelica's voice was so kind, so sympathetic.

"Well, it's like Robert and Nicole... are still hurting me in a way," Erin stammered. She pressed her hands onto Talent's withers to stop them from shaking. "I feel as if they damaged something in me, something deep inside. Not my bones or anything, but something in my heart, in my mind." Her voice quavered as she confided in her new friend. "I feel like I never want to leave home again, and I know that's not good. What if I never get over this fear, Angelica? What if I'm never brave again?"

"They can not hurt you now, Erin. And soon they will be in jail."

"You're right. I know you're right," she said, though her heart was thudding madly in her chest.

"I am so sorry this happened to you, Erin," Angelica whispered.

Talent whinnied again and turned his head to nuzzle Erin's foot. Unable to control her tremors, she leaned forward to lie over his neck. Breathe in his scent. Would she ever dare to ride alone again? Or even go to school? Or visit her friends?

"Do you mind, Erin, if I ask you a question?" Angelica said behind her.

"Of course not," said Erin, knowing Angelica was probably trying to distract her from her fear yet again.

"It is so open around the castle. I was expecting it to be more protected, with obvious ways for Nicole and Robert to approach unseen. However, there is only barren flat land around the ruins. Are they just going to drive up to the castle, when the police can easily lie in wait for them and capture them? It does not seem a very good plan."

Erin straightened, forced herself to look toward the ruins. "It doesn't make much sense, does it? I wonder…" She gasped. She had just remembered something, something that made her blood run cold. Nicole and Robert wouldn't be going to jail because the police wouldn't catch them.

"No, Angelica," she managed to choke out. "And they won't be caught. Because I made a mistake. A horrible, horrible mistake. I messed everything up."

"What do you mean, Erin?" Angelica sounded so calm and reasonable. How could she?

"Because," Erin said, her voice overflowing with dread. "I forgot something. I heard them talking. They have a secret way in and out of the castle, through a sea cave. The castle is on the edge of the ocean, you see? And when they realize that Dad didn't leave any real money, Nicole will be so angry. She'll come after me, Angelica. I just know she will!"

Erin held her breath as she waited for Angelica to speak. She deserved to be rebuked, and worse. How could she forget such important information? Of course, at the time, her head was hurting so much it was almost impossible to concentrate on anything else, but that was no excuse. She should have remembered.

"Erin, I think you and Talent should go on to the stonecutter's cottages and wait there for your father," Angelica finally said.

Erin released her breath in an explosion of relief, and quickly nodded her agreement. Angelica slipped from Talent's back. "You'll be careful, right, Angelica?" she asked, looking down at the older girl. Instantly, she felt such an overwhelming rush of guilt that she didn't register Angelica's answer. How could she let her new friend finish this for her? How could she abandon Angelica like this? But could she summon enough courage to go with her? And what if she had to face the kidnappers again? Would they try to recapture her? Or worse, hurt her? Erin unsuccessfully tried to blink back her tears.

"Please, do not worry. I will do my best," said Angelica. When Erin didn't answer, she continued in a comforting voice. "And I will see you again soon. I will come to the stone cutters' cottages afterwards to tell you what happened, and to say goodbye."

"But I *can't* let you do it alone," Erin's voice was almost a wail. "I *have* to help you."

Angelica was silent for a moment, and when she spoke her voice echoed with relief. "I must admit that I am glad to hear you say that. I think this may be the way to heal yourself of your fear, Erin. Sometimes the only way is to step forward when we think we can not, and to do what we are too afraid to do." She touched the younger girl's arm gently. "And I will do my best to keep you safe, little one."

The words sounded so strange coming from someone barely older than she was, but they were oddly comforting — as if Angelica was thousands of years old instead of sixteen or seventeen. As if there were even stranger things about her than hair that could change color and hands that could heal. As if an entire world of wisdom was living behind her golden eyes. "Angelica? Who are you?" Erin whispered. She rubbed away the tears from her face.

A soft smile touched the ivory face. "I am Angelica, helper of horses and their loved ones. That is all."

"Where are you from? Really, you can tell me," said Erin, grateful for the diversion.

"You would not believe me," said Angelica, her amber eyes locked on Erin's.

"Please, tell me anyway."

"I am from the wind, Erin, from the light, from the breath of the Great One. I am from the brightness of moon and the music of stars singing in the darkness. I am from the hopes and wishes and loves of all horses, past, present, and future. I am…" She stopped, searched Erin's startled face, and then smiled serenely. "I am your friend, Erin. And I will sacrifice myself before I let anything happen to you or to Talent. That I hope you believe."

"I do," Erin said without hesitation. "And the other…

stuff… you said. I believe that too. I just don't understand it."

Angelica leapt up behind her onto Talent's bare back. "That is because I can not explain it well." She paused. "Are you sure you want to do this Erin?"

Erin nodded. "I want to be brave again, Angelica. I don't want to spend the rest of my life being afraid."

"I am glad. So let us make our plan."

Erin stroked Talent's neck as she thought. They didn't seem to have many options. "There's no time left to find a payphone to let Dad know, and we can't wait on the road and flag down the police to tell them, because they're probably already there, hiding. We can't ride up to the castle because the kidnappers might see us and run off."

"Then there is only one thing we can do to make sure the kidnappers are captured."

"Yes," said Erin. She struggled to speak for a moment, and when the words came out they sounded thin and brittle. "We have to go into the cave and make sure they don't leave it."

"If we hurry, we can lock their secret entrance after they go through to get the money," said Angelica. "Then they will be trapped above with the police officers." She sounded so confident.

Erin straightened on Talent's back. *I can pretend to be as confident, if nothing else. Maybe pretending to be brave will make me less afraid.* "Okay," she said, her voice full of false bravado. "Let's do it."

The drive to the parking lot beside the beach had been uneventful. The sun seemed only inches above the sea when they started their trek along the sands. Soon the sand changed to pebbles, which gave way in time to stones. The dunes at the back of the beach rose higher and higher, turned to dirt, then to rock. The rocky beach narrowed until it was a slender wedge between the ocean and the cliff, and then it became narrower still.

Nicole was about to ask how much farther, when she noticed the dark gash in the cliff ahead. The slit was well over their heads, and thin. It had to be the entrance to the underground passage.

Robert strode past without hesitation.

"Where are you going?" asked Nicole, all the frustration from the last two days packed into her voice.

"That's not the right cave," Robert replied, without looking back.

With a clenched jaw, Nicole followed him.

The beach continued to narrow until there were only a couple of feet between the cliff and the ocean, and then they were in the water. A wave splashed over Nicole's shoes, soaking them instantly. She gasped — it was freezing cold! The next wave was up to her knees.

"It's getting too deep," she complained, even though she knew she'd swim if she had to.

"The tide's going out soon," replied Robert. "It'll be lower when we leave."

They continued to splash through the water. A huge boulder leaned against the cliff in front of them, looking as if it had fallen from above. "It's right past this rock," said Robert. "We have to walk around to get to the entrance. Do you want me to carry you?"

"No, I can manage." The water was halfway up her thighs now. And here came another wave. The wave rolled past her, wetting her to her waist, then crashed against the boulder and sprayed back over her. It took all her self-control to not shriek at the icy shower. As quickly as she could, she edged the rest of the way around the boulder and crept up onto the thin sliver of beach rocks on the other side, shivering. "Where is it?" she demanded.

"Right here," Robert said, gesturing to the dark hole beside the rock.

Nicole pulled her flashlight from her pocket and shone it on the sea cave entrance. "Are you sure?"

"Positive," said Robert. When Nicole hesitated to enter the cavern, he added, "Don't worry. I'll go first." He walked in through the cave entrance, and Nicole hurried to follow.

Talent cantered carefully across the Burren toward the sea, the two girls light on his back. Their plan was to gallop along the beach to the cliff below the ruins, where they hoped to find the sea cave. The ground became rougher as they neared the ocean, the gaps between the pavements more pronounced, the evening darker. By the time they reached the beach, night was falling. Without hesitation, Talent turned onto the broad strip of sand and increased his speed. Now they could really make up some time.

"They came this way more than half an hour ago," said Angelica.

"How can you tell?" A new moon hung in the sky before them.

"I have the ability to track other beings, even though much of their passing has been erased by the rising tide."

"Do you know how much higher will it get?"

"It will soon be at its peak."

The beach was becoming narrower now, and Talent slowed to a canter. Then when the water met the cliff, he broke into a trot that became higher and bouncier as the water became deeper. Moon glow skipped and flashed silver all around them.

"There!" said Erin, between bounces. She unclasped Talent's mane with one hand and pointed at the dark slit in the cliff face in front of them.

"They went past this one, I think," said Angelica, though she didn't sound too sure of herself. "I can not be certain, for the water's wave energy has disrupted much of their trail, but I believe we must go farther."

"But…" Erin didn't want to say it. Angelica might be insulted.

"But what?"

"But aren't… their tracks… totally… wiped out?" Talent chose this moment to slow to a walk and Erin's speech returned to normal. "The water is almost to Tallie's knees. How can you track them?"

"I am not tracking them by imprints left in the sand, but by their energy," Angelica clarified.

Erin didn't know what to say. It was a bizarre skill — but Angelica hadn't led them wrong yet. Talent too seemed happy to be passing the sea cave entrance.

A huge boulder lay in front of them, completely blocking the shallower water. "It's so deep," said Erin and pulled her feet out of the water's reach as Talent walked around the massive rock. "Do you think that'll stop the kidnappers from escaping from the cave?"

"I think they will swim if they have to, to get away. The waves are not too rough tonight and it would be easy to do, although very cold."

"Look," Erin said in a dread-filled voice. She pointed. There it was — the sea cave. Even she could tell it was the right one because someone had recently gone inside. She could see their wet tracks glistening in the moonlight where they'd walked through the opening. This was it. Could she do it?

She shrank back against Angelica as Talent splashed toward the cave mouth. It was so dark, like a black hole in space that trapped light and life, and extinguished it.

"Do not worry. We will be able to see," Angelica whispered behind her as Talent walked into the cave.

And they could, even though Erin didn't see how it was possible. The light wasn't coming from anywhere in particular. Instead, it seemed to be hanging in the air all around them, illuminating everything just enough that their passage was safe. Talent wove through the rocky spires and boulders, around tidal pools and along ledges, the sound of his hooves strangely muffled. Was he stepping on seaweed? Erin looked down. No! His hooves were encased in light!

"Angelica!" Immediately, Erin bit down on her lip. She'd been far too loud.

"I know," whispered the older girl. "It is nothing to worry about."

Erin nodded, and looked down again. Maybe the cave was home to colonies of miniscule luminous sea creatures. She'd heard of strange things like this before. And it could explain the strange source of light that seemed to hang in the air as well. They were only brighter against Talent's hooves because he was touching them. And they were muting the sound of his steps too. How fortunate!

A distant laugh shot from around the corner ahead of them and Erin jerked erect. She'd recognize that laugh anywhere — Robert! Then she recognized Nicole's voice, speaking just a short word or two.

"It's them," Erin hissed and shrank back against Angelica again. The scrape of boots against stones sent her trembling uncontrollably. They were coming closer! They'd already picked up what they thought was the money, and were making their getaway! "Angelica? What do we do?"

"Trust me," the girl whispered insistently in her ear. "I have an idea. Wait until I tell you to go forward, then ride Talent toward them." She slid from the gelding's back.

Instantly, the light from the luminous creatures vanished, all except those around Talent's hooves. Panic stricken, Erin looked back. Where had Angelica gone? The girl was nowhere to be seen. But she wouldn't just abandon Erin and Talent.

Would she?

Nicole felt so light, so alive! What a rush this whole thing had been! Now that it was over, and they had the money, all the problems they'd experienced seemed to melt away. She was rich again! Once more, she was a wealthy, wealthy woman! She could have anything she wanted! Anything! And all they had left to do was walk out of the cave, stroll along the beach pretending to be tourists out for a starlit walk, and then jump in their car and go.

But, wait. There was one more thing. She had to decide what to do with the girl. Once they were safely away, should she phone the girl's father? Or not?

She had to make the right decision. It could mean the difference between a privileged life and prison.

Erin couldn't move. The stab of light from the kidnapper's flashlight grew longer, danced closer, as the seconds passed. Any moment they would walk around the corner and see her and Talent.

"I'm sorry, Angelica. I can't do it," she whispered. She touched Talent's side in an attempt to turn him.

"Erin, trust me. I am right here behind you."

Erin looked back but could see no one.

"Remember, I will take care of you." Angelica's whisper flowed from the darkness. "Now watch."

Erin turned back to face the advancing flashlight beam. So this was when either her courage would win out or she would become a coward, completely. She could hear the scrape of boots on stone. Hear their words. Nicole was telling Robert what they were going to buy with their money. They didn't know yet that they'd been tricked. Words like condo, and Paris, and sports car floated around the corner, and as Erin heard them, a strange feeling began to spread through her chest and head. White hot anger.

How could they terrorize her for a sports car? For a condo? For a trip to Paris? How could her safety and freedom be worth so little? Had they even thought of her at all since walking away from the tomb? She could be dead right now for all they knew, and here they were, gloating over non-existent prizes.

Erin heard a gurgling behind her and looked back. Water was flowing into the cave, dark and swift. Talent's softly glowing hooves were under the water now and it was climbing rapidly up his forelegs. Then lowering. How odd!

Look ahead. Angelica's voice sounded through her mind.

Erin turned to face forward, and gasped! The ocean water was at Talent's eye height and rising, a thin tidal wall. Her hand stroked his trembling shoulder. "Don't be scared, Tallie," she whispered. "It's Angelica's magic." The horse snorted softly in reply. He already knew.

The two kidnappers rounded the corner. Erin sat perfectly still as she watched them pick their way through the rocks toward her, laughing, with their eyes on the uneven ground. They hadn't seen the rising wall of water yet, almost high enough now to hide Erin and Talent.

Move forward. Angelica's voice.

This was it. This was the time to choose. Go toward them? Or run away.

And suddenly, in her heart Erin knew there was only one choice. She couldn't run. If she did, she would never be able to stop running. From her kidnappers, because she was a witness. From people who might tease her. From anything that went wrong in her life or anyone who wasn't kind to her. She would end up running all her life. And she would never become the person she was meant to be.

The choice finally made, Erin nudged Talent's sides with her heels. "Let's go, boy," she said quietly, her words barely audible. "Let's get them."

Tell them how you feel, when the light flashes. Loudly.

Despite herself, Erin smiled. Maybe this could even be fun.

133

"What's that?"

Nicole almost ran into Robert, he stopped so quickly. "What?" she asked, feeling her irritation return immediately. What was wrong now?

"That noise," said Robert. "Don't you hear it?"

"It's just water."

"But the tide was close to its peak when we came in," explained Robert. "I checked the tide charts. It shouldn't be coming into the cave."

Nicole flashed her light farther ahead of them. "I see something." Then the light illuminated… no, it was impossible. She had to be seeing things.

"It looks like a waterfall," whispered Robert. "A frozen waterfall. But not really frozen. Just… still."

Fear lurched into Nicole's heart. If Robert saw it too, her mind wasn't playing tricks on her. It had to be real.

"How do we get past it?" asked Robert, his voice shaking.

Nicole inhaled sharply when a rock disappeared behind the wall of water. "It's moving toward us," she whispered, horror-struck.

Suddenly, a bright light came from inside the water — and etched in solid darkness in the middle of the flat expanse was a shadow of a girl on a horse.

"You hurt me!" The speaker sounded as if she were yelling from underwater. Then the light vanished.

"It's her!" Robert shrieked. "It's Erin. She died, and now she's coming to get us!" He stumbled backward. "I'm sorry. I'm so sorry, Erin! Please forgive me. I didn't mean to hurt you. I should have listened to you. I'm sorry, so very, very sorry!"

Nicole's flashlight clattered to the ground, went out, and the sudden darkness was beyond horrible. She couldn't see where the still waterfall was. Robert was sobbing in the background, begging for forgiveness, and totally useless. Nicole dropped to her hands and knees and felt desperately for the flashlight.

The bright flash came again and Nicole looked up in horror, to see the wall of water even closer to them. The silhouetted girl and her horse were just yards away.

"I needed water. Water. Why didn't you give me more? I'm thirsty," the girl gargled again. The light extinguished as quickly as it appeared.

However, Nicole had seen her flashlight in the sudden burst. She grabbed for it, clicked it on, shone it on the advancing wall. It was even closer. How was this happening? She spun around and hurried to Robert's side. "Get up!" Her voice was shrill with panic. "There has to be another way out of here!"

Her brother shook his head, his eyes locked on the advancing wall behind her.

The flash came again, along with the hideous watery voice. "You locked me in a tomb, and night came. You promised I'd be home by dark. Why aren't I home? Where's my family? I'm so thirsty!"

"Come on!" Nicole screamed to Robert, grabbed his arm, and jerked. She knew now what they had to do. He had to get up. They had to run, and run together. She wasn't about to leave him here to be drowned — or something infinitely worse.

Erin was as surprised as the kidnappers when the first flash of light came, so the first thing she said was short and simple. However, the effect it had, with Angelica's powers behind it, was truly amazing. Robert was immediately reduced to a helpless lump.

By the time the second flash came Erin was better prepared, and by the third flash, she was completely enjoying herself. Finally, she was getting her revenge on her kidnappers! And she didn't even have to be mean to them as they'd been to her. She was merely throwing their own actions back in their faces.

When Nicole finally got Robert to his feet, grabbed the bag of fake money he'd dropped, and pushed her brother down the passage away from the advancing water wall, Erin almost cheered. She'd seen Robert shake his head when Nicole asked him about another way out of the cave. That meant only one thing. The only way out was back the way they'd come, through the castle where they'd picked up their money. Where the police waited.

We must hurry. I am losing power.

"Angelica, are you okay?" Would the girl even hear her?

Hurry.

The wall of water picked up speed, moving after Robert and Nicole. Erin encouraged Talent to move faster behind it. If Angelica was losing strength, they did indeed have to hurry.

"Faster, Tallie." She could hear Talent's hooves on the rocks now, not loud but still she could hear them. The light wasn't muffling his step as it had been. Hopefully it wasn't far to the castle.

Talent clattered quickly behind the wall of water. Every now and then Erin caught the sound of voices ahead. The kidnappers were still running. And she couldn't blame them. Her and Tallie's shadows darkening the bright wall of water must make a terrifying picture.

They turned another corner, to see the kidnappers against the far wall of a dead end chamber.

"Slow the water down, Angelica," Erin whispered, hoping the girl could hear her. "Slow down, Tallie." Her fingers stroked his neck and she leaned back slightly, moved her heels away from his side.

Talent snorted, and in the breathless silence that followed, Angelica's light flashed again, much less powerful, much softer. And the wall of water was lower. The magic was disappearing. Erin had to make this good.

"You tried to steal my life," she moaned, and was very grateful to notice that her voice still sounded watery.

With spastic movements, Robert began to climb. Erin hadn't seen the rusty ladder behind them. Her eyes traveled upward. About ten feet up was a trap door. The entrance to the castle!

Somehow, she needed to scare them up the ladder and into the castle. If they were panicky when they went through the trap door, the police should hear them, and then arrest them.

And she and Talent would be left here below. Without Angelica's light. Alone.

How much longer can I hold the tide in place? How much longer can I keep the glowing? It becomes harder as they move farther from me.

I am so tired.

And suddenly, I feel another calling me for help! And here I am — without even the energy to help Erin and Talent for much longer.

Can you hear me, Tango? I will come to you as soon as I am able.

If I am able.

Nicole followed Robert up the first few rungs of the ladder but had to stop when he reached the top. And he was showing no signs of going through the trap door. What was he thinking? That he'd be safe, being the highest on the ladder? That the ghosts and the water would only get her?

She looked down at the water fearfully. The wall was shortening. And it was glowing softly now. The ghosts were silent. Why? Were they laying some horrible trap?

And then she saw it – a dark spot in the water wall, which turned to a horse's nose, and then a blazed face.

"Were you going to tell them where to find me?" the watery voice asked.

The entire horse's head was through now, and now its neck. The rider's pale hands, drenched head. Dark stone eyes stared into Nicole's as if they could see to the bottom of her soul.

"You weren't, were you?" the ghost said.

"I was. I promise," stammered Nicole.

But the ghost could see she was lying. And suddenly it was glowing too! "There are always consequences to our actions," it said, its voice an underwater scream. Then it reached for Nicole with a white hand. Reached.

And Nicole lost all control. The duffle bag thudded to the floor of the sea cave, and with jerky, panicked movements, she grabbed Robert's pant legs and started to climb.

Erin tried to keep the smile off her face as she watched Nicole literally climb up Robert's body. It felt wonderful to see this woman, who had terrorized her so completely, lose control. Nicole opened the trapdoor so fast that it fell back against the floor of the abandoned castle with a loud clang, and then she was through and out of sight. Robert was only milliseconds behind her, whispering loudly at her to wait for him.

With incredible satisfaction, Erin put a hand on each side of her mouth, cupped like a loudspeaker and yelled, "Dad! Dad! The kidnapper's are in the castle! Dad! Dad! Dad!"

The trapdoor slammed shut. The kidnappers were trying to shut off her voice. Erin continued to stare upward. Muffled footsteps echoed through the chamber. Then she heard yelling. The sound of a scuffle over her head. Were the kidnappers being taken into custody? Or were they escaping? She waited breathlessly in the semi darkness.

A sound came from behind her, soft gurgling. Erin spun around on Talent's back. The water was losing its structure. It was spreading out, splashing across the floor, a knee-deep pond, now that Angelica's power had released it. Some of it settled in the low spots of the chamber, but most of it ran back along the passageway, flowing out to the sea.

"Angelica?" The glowing was quickly receding. Erin was totally back to normal, though very wet, and Talent was dark beneath her. "Angelica? Are you there? Can you hear me?"

No answer. Not even in her head.

"Angelica! Angelica!" Was she okay? Or was she just too far away to hear Erin's voice? Or had something happened to her back in the cave?

Had she drowned?

There was a rasping noise overhead, and Erin looked up to see the trapdoor open. A flashlight beam illuminated the cave. "Erin, is that you?"

"Dad!" Erin slid from Talent's back and splashed as quickly as she could to the ladder. Moments later, her father's strong, warm arms were around her.

Erin was only above ground for a couple of minutes before she knew she needed to get back to Talent and Angelica. Now that the kidnappers were caught, she had to find Angelica and help Talent from the sea cave. Quickly, she explained to her dad about Talent in the cave. Angelica, she decided, she would introduce when they found her — if they found her. And if not, she would keep Angelica's secret as she'd sworn.

Her dad was happy to accompany her into the sea cave. In fact, Erin knew there was no way he would let her go alone. He probably wasn't going to let her out of his sight for a while. They splashed ankle deep in seawater at the bottom of the ladder, and the powerful flashlights they'd gotten from the police officers brightened the interior. The chamber was empty.

"Tallie?" called Erin. When there was no answering neigh, she looked up at her dad. "He must have already started out," she said, trying to keep the concern from her voice.

"Don't worry, Erin. He couldn't have gone far in the dark," her dad reassured her. "We'll find this miracle horse of yours."

"This is the way out. Follow me," Erin said, and started down the passage to the sea.

Talent, you have come to save me. I thank you for your tears of love, your beautiful, healing tears.

My energy is returning. My spark is becoming stronger.

Talent, another called me while I was helping you and Erin. His name is Tango and he needs me. And so I must go.

Thank you again, my dear, for saving me. I am so sorry to rush away.

Until we meet again, fare well.

Erin tried to answer her dad's questions as she flashed her light around the cave, looking for Talent and Angelica. She told him how the kidnappers caught her and pinned the note to Talent's saddle pad, of the hikers they'd passed, and of trekking across the Burren at night.

She'd just gotten to her attempt to escape the night before, when her flashlight beam illuminated a red horse. "Tallie!" Erin rushed forward. When she reached him, he nickered and lowered his muzzle into her hands.

"Tallie? Where's Angelica?" she whispered low enough that her dad couldn't hear.

The horse raised his head to nuzzle a high rocky shelf in the cave wall.

"This is where she stayed above the water?" questioned Erin. "But where is she now?"

Talent's ears flicked forward. He was looking behind her now. Her dad was approaching.

When the man reached the horse, he stood still for a moment and reverently reached out and ran his hand along Talent's cheek. Then, with his expression full of emotion, he threw his arms around Talent's neck. Finally, he turned to Erin and pulled her close. She felt him bend over and kiss the top of her head. A sob broke the silence of the sea cave.

"I'm okay now, Dad," she said, and patted his back in an

effort to comfort him. "And the kidnappers are caught now. Everything's okay."

"Erin, I am so sorry I wasn't able to protect you. It's my job to keep you safe. Please, please, forgive me."

Erin didn't know what to say. None of this had been her dad's fault. How could he think it was?

"I let you down yesterday," her dad continued. "And not only by not protecting you from the kidnappers, but for not being more understanding after Siobhan's play. I thought that was why you were gone for so long. I thought you needed time away from us all. I didn't realize you'd been kidnapped. And then we got that note..." He swallowed noisily. "If I'd stopped you from going off, if I'd made us all sit down and have a family conference or something, you never would have been kidnapped. I am so, so sorry!"

"Dad, listen, it's *not* your fault. Not one little bit. Robert and Nicole were waiting for me. If they hadn't grabbed me yesterday, they would've just tried another day. Nicole is a mean sociopath, Dad. She doesn't care about anyone or anything, except herself, and you certainly didn't make her that way."

He pulled away and looked down at her. "What did you say?"

"It's *not* your fault."

"The other part."

"That Nicole's a mean sociopath?"

A tiny smile slipped onto his face. "That's what I thought you said." Self-consciously he wiped the tears from his face. "That's all Sylvie and I need: another psychiatrist in the family. All we've been hearing since yesterday afternoon is the psychological profiles of kidnappers. Siobhan was worried sick about you and it was the only thing she could think to do to help. It was enough to drive a person mad."

146

Erin rolled her eyes. "Believe me, I know what you mean."

Her dad's smile disappeared. "Are you sure you're okay, Erin?"

She nodded. "I am." And she was. That was the amazing thing. Facing her fear, confronting the kidnappers and watching them turn into gibbering idiots, had been just the medicine she needed to conquer her fear. "I'm just tired, that's all," she added.

"Here, let me help you mount." He lifted her onto the big horse's back.

"Do you want to ride too?"

"No, I can walk." He tugged on Talent's mane. When the gelding looked at him with a curious expression on his elegant face, Erin laughed.

"Don't worry, Dad, I know how to direct him."

"Even without a bridle?"

Erin touched Talent with her heels and the horse stepped obediently forward. "It's not as hard as it seems," she said, looking back. "If your horse knows leg aids, that is, which Tallie certainly does."

She flashed her light into every nook and cranny as she rode. Luckily the sea cave was relatively straight and there weren't many hidden spots. The water had left pools here and there and Erin found them the hardest to check. What if Angelica's ledge hadn't been high enough and the tide had drowned her? What if she found the beautiful, strange girl floating in one of the pools? She couldn't bear it if Angelica died, especially if it happened while she was saving Erin. She just had to be all right!

All too soon, they were at the cave opening. The tide had receded somewhat and they walked out onto the rock beach and around the big boulder without getting any wetter. Then they began their long trek along the ocean. Erin was glad her dad wasn't asking her any more questions. Her saying she was tired had apparently made him decide to wait to get the rest of the story.

The rocks beneath their feet turned to pebbles, the pebbles to sand, and then Erin could see the parking lot ahead of them, just behind the beach. Car lights, she assumed, from police cars, and a small crowd of people were in the parking lot, waiting for them.

At the edge of the parking lot, the trio stopped. "You can wait here if you want, Erin. I'll tell them I'm taking you to the hospital, and then home for some rest. They'll want to talk to you tomorrow though, okay?"

Erin was relieved. She didn't feel up to telling the story tonight. Not when she didn't know how it would end. "Okay." When her dad strode away, Erin leaned forward to rest across Talent's withers. Slowly, she stroked his neck. "Where is she, Tallie?" she whispered. "How can we find her?"

Erin.

Talent raised his head and Erin sat bolt upright. "Angelica?" she said, too loud. She looked toward the group of men and women near the cars. Two people glanced her way, and then hurried toward her. "Angelica," she said again, quietly. "Can you hear me?"

I had to go help another who needed me. But I left something for you.

There was a sudden tingling against her little finger and Erin looked down. Something was glimmering there in the light, something caught in Talent's mane. She reached down and pulled it free. It was a long golden hair.

Suddenly, the hair glowed with light. Warmth spread along Erin's fingers, to her hand, to her arm. She was so

148

surprised she almost dropped the single strand, but then the tingling ceased. The hair quivered.

And it was a hair no longer. It was a necklace! The most beautiful necklace Erin had ever seen!

When you need me, touch the necklace and call my name. I will hear you then, and come to you.

"Thank you," Erin whispered, though the words seemed so inadequate. Angelica had saved her life and helped her face her fears. And now she'd left her this necklace as a lifeline in case anything bad ever happened again. Now Erin *really* never needed to feel afraid again. How could she ever express enough gratitude?

And I thank you and Talent too.

Erin smiled sadly. It was just like Angelica to turn her words around. How she was going to miss her! Tears prickled her eyes. "But if nothing goes wrong, I'll never see you again. I don't want to say goodbye."

To you then, my friend, I will not say goodbye. Instead, I will say fare well, Erin, until the next time we meet. And we will meet again. Without any kidnappers being involved.

Talent snorted, and Erin could hear Angelica's laugh flow around her on the night breeze, soft and musical.

Erin smiled. "Fare well, Angelica," she said loudly, not caring anymore if anyone heard her. Let them *all* think she was crazy. "Fare extremely well."

"I knew she'd break under the pressure, Mum. She's gone insane."

Erin looked back to see Siobhan and Sylvie walk the last few steps toward her and Talent. She slid from the gelding's back and was immediately engulfed in Sylvie's hug. "Oh, Erin. Oh, Erin," was all her stepmom could say before she burst into tears.

Erin hugged her back as hard as she could. "I'm so glad to be home."

"You're not home. You're in a parking lot," corrected Siobhan.

"You're wrong," said Erin, when Sylvie released her. "I'm home when I'm with Dad and Sylvie." She smiled into her stepmom's eyes, then turned to her stepsister. "And you too, Siobhan."

The moonlight illuminated a tentative smile on Siobhan's face. "I'm glad you're home too," she finally said.

"I'll be back in a minute, sweetheart," said Sylvie, stroking Erin's hair. "I'll call to see if your riding instructor will come to give Talent a ride home in her horse trailer, okay?"

"Thanks, Sylvie." Erin watched her stepmom walk away, then looked down at the ground. Now that she was alone with Siobhan, it was probably a good time to tell her how she regretted her unkind comment about Siobhan's play. "I'm sorry," she blurted out, and then looked up, surprised. Siobhan had said she was sorry at exactly the same moment! "What are you sorry for?" asked Erin. "You didn't say anything mean."

"Oh, just for being such a pain and trying to get on your nerves."

"You're pretty good at that," Erin admitted with a grin.

Siobhan gave her a lopsided smile. "Thanks. It's one of my talents."

"I want to thank you too," added Erin.

"For what?"

"For being such a pain and spouting psycho stuff all the time. It helped out there, a couple of times, in fact."

"Glad to be of service," said Siobhan.

Talent whinnied, and stepped toward Siobhan, his ears pricked forward. Instinctively, Siobhan stepped back.

"He won't hurt you," said Erin. "I promise." She stroked

151

the gelding's cheek. "He's the best horse in the world. He saved me."

"I know. It's just he's so big and…"

"Hey, you have equine-phobia!" interrupted Erin, laughing. "You're an equinephobe."

"No, I'm not!"

"Really? Then prove it."

"Okay. I will." Siobhan reached cautiously to touch the gelding's face. Jerked her fingers away. Reached out again. "Hey, he's soft. And silky."

Talent nickered and reached out to nuzzle her, and Siobhan laughed when he tickled her neck.

"So what's this?" said Erin's dad as he approached, Sylvie beside him. "Siobhan likes horses too now?"

"She's a reformed equinephobe," offered Erin.

Siobhan looked sideways at Erin, winked, then turned to face their parents. "Mum, can I have a horse too? Not one to ride, but one to take care of? One that needs me."

Instantly, Erin realized what Siobhan was up to, and she wasn't about to let the opportunity pass by. This was the perfect solution for Magic — having Siobhan pamper him. "And I know just the horse for her," she added quickly. "You remember me asking about Magic? Well, he's the sweetest horse you'll ever meet, except for Tallie, of course."

"Well, I think Magic's even sweeter than Tallie," said Siobhan in her snobby voice. "In fact, I'm thoroughly positive he is."

Sylvie rolled her eyes. "Great, *more* competition!"

"Just like sisters," said Siobhan.

"Just like sisters," Erin confirmed with a grin.

David, I hear you. I am coming.

Are you here?

I see no one.

The old house and overgrown yard are completely dark. The fields are neglected and only one small shed remains, but I recognize this place. There was a barn here once, and well-manicured fields. The house was painted and the horses who lived here were healthy and happy. This is where I once assisted Dancer. Wings and Rocket Gal lived here too then. However, that was long ago. They would all be gone now.

Though the yard is empty, I am sure this is the place from which David called me. But where is he now?

I will unite with Tango. He is nearby, in that small shed. I can sense his summons still, though it is not strong as it once was. His emergency is over. I feel dreadful that I could not go to him earlier, when he needed me. But there is nothing I can do about that now, other than my best to right what has been wronged.

And maybe his crisis is related to David's. Maybe I can help them both.